Seduction AND SURRENDER

The Billionaire's Temptation Series

Cali MacKay

Seduction and Surrender
The Billionaire's Temptation Series
By Cali MacKay

Published by Daeron Publishing

http://calimackay.com

Printed in the United States of America

First Printing, 2014, edition 1.0

ISBN: 978-1-940041-28-5

For Joe, Maeve and Amelia.

I'd also like to thank all my readers, critique partners and betas for their invaluable support and all their help.

For more information or to join a mailing list for updates, please visit http://calimackay.com.

Seduction

AND SURRENDER

T HE KNIFE WAS A BLUR in Emma's hand as she chopped the onions for the night's service, her prep cook having left her in the lurch again. She tried to be understanding of true emergencies, but getting too drunk the night before wasn't a valid excuse for missing work the following morning—yet again. And of all the days to be short-staffed.

"You need to get going, Em. Leave it. I'll finish that up." Jake shouldered her out of the way and took over the prep she was working on. "And make sure you take a shower before going to that meeting. Ryker will never agree to extend the lease if you smell like onions and a butcher's."

She wiped her hands on a rag, her mind racing and her stomach in knots as her nerves got the best of her. Formal meetings of any sort always put her on edge, especially when there was so much at stake. "I swear, I could kiss you. Thanks. I owe you, big time."

He shook his head with a sigh and a teasing smile, his brown eyes lighting up. "Promises, promises."

With a wave, Emma grabbed her bag and rushed out the door, quickly checking the time on her phone as she fumbled with her keys. If she hurried, she'd just make it. And there was no way she could be late. The fate of her restaurant depended on this meeting being a success. If she couldn't get her lease renewed, she'd lose everything—and it wasn't just her life's savings and her restaurant that were on the line.

Letting herself into her studio apartment, she quickly stripped and turned on the hot water. Her shower spit to life, the pipes clanging and stuttering before releasing a weak spray of warm water. She cursed her landlord and the hot water heater that seldom delivered actual hot water, and stepped in for a quick shower. At least the temperature guaranteed she wouldn't linger.

Between the towel and blow-drier, she managed to half-dry her hair before pulling it back into one of her no-nonsense ponytails, and since she didn't have much in the way of fancy clothes, a pair of skinny cream pants and a silky pink tunic would just have to do. She looked at her shoes and cringed. No way could she wear her go-to work clogs, but there was a good chance she'd kill herself in heels. She groaned, knowing she had little choice and already regretting her decision as she squeezed her feet into the silver pumps she'd bought when she was a bridesmaid for her cousin's wedding.

She slicked some gloss across her full lips, and jogged out the door, nearly killing herself in the process, and already running five minutes late. Of course, traffic was miserable with tourists filling the town to go foliage peeping, only adding to how late she was. There just better be parking when she finally got there.

There wasn't.

By the time she found a place to park, she was three blocks away from where she needed to be. Kicking off her heels, she hightailed it barefoot to the fancy high-rise that housed the offices of Ryker Investments, and one Quinn Ryker. Thankfully, the residents of Portmore kept their city fairly clean, or she'd have had to add stitches and a tetanus shot to her list of things to do that day.

With her pulse thrumming, she rushed through the glass doors and across the marble floor, thinking it was a damn good thing she was still barefoot. Those floors would have been her demise if she'd been wearing her heels. Twelfth floor, but no suite was listed. She just hoped it'd be obvious once she got up there. She spotted the elevator about to go up.

"Hold the elevator, please!" Emma practically dove in between the closing doors—and right into a wall of hard muscles and the arms of a total stranger.

With her heart now racing for a completely different reason, her gaze wandered across a broad chest, all the way up to sexy stubble on a strong jawline, and dark mussed-up hair that made the stranger's eyes stand out in contrast—mesmerizing, intelligent eyes the color of spring grass. The man was heart-stoppingly gorgeous in a rugged animalistic way, and so damn tall, that his presence left her feeling tiny and delicate, even if she'd never before thought of herself in those terms.

She managed to suck a breath into her lungs while still in the stranger's arms, gripping his massive biceps through his worn leather biker jacket, butter soft with age and wear. Yet the way he was built, and the ease with which he carried his large frame, made her think that his muscles were the kind earned through hard work rather than the gym—and damn, but she'd love nothing more than to see those muscles in action.

He looked down at her with one eyebrow lifted in question as she all but blushed, though she made no move to extricate herself from his muscular arms, her brain and body clearly having fried themselves due to his close proximity. And it sure as hell didn't help that he smelled like leather, fresh ocean air, and pure man.

"*Sorry.*" What the hell was her problem? "So incredibly sorry."

Juggling her, in addition to his motorcycle helmet, the man easily shifted her back onto her feet as if he were used to having to free himself from crazy women. His lips twitched into a hint of a smile that nearly made her heart stutter and sent a blush flaming across her cheeks. "No worries, sweetheart. You won't ever hear me complain about having a pretty woman fling herself into my arms."

Emma suspected it was likely a common occurrence, given that the man was smoking hot, in a way that few men were. He had a presence that demanded attention, like a feral creature so rare and dangerous, one couldn't help but look in awe. And the fact that he easily stood over six foot three only added to it.

Snap out of it, Emma! The man was probably thinking she was off her rocker.

She forced herself to take a deep breath, her thoughts slowly returning to normal as if her brain was finally starting to function now that there was a bit of distance between them. Remembering why she was there, she pressed the button for the twelfth floor.

Shoes! She stepped into one of them, and then attempted to get the second one on while balancing on the spindly heel of the first.

Just as she was about to go down again, her handsome stranger reached out and steadied her with a hand on her waist, his fingers pressing firmly into her flesh. His touch, the command in his hold, sent a jolt of electricity through to her core and reminded her that it had been *far too long* since she'd last been with a man. And this man? She had no doubt he was capable of mind-blowing, knee-weakening, *When-Harry-Met-Sally* types of orgasms.

His eyes locked on hers for a moment before wandering to her lips, and then over her entire body, his smile kicking up as his gaze lingered over her curves. "Are you going to be all right, sweetheart?"

Sweetheart... The way he said that word made her heart skitter.

Still wobbly, she finally managed to get the second shoe on, though she didn't attempt to pull out of his arms, since the last thing she wanted was to sprawl at the feet of this man-god. "Sorry. Again."

"You're not going to go down in a heap if I let you go, are you?" His brow kicked up questioningly, sending her heart racing.

"It's these heels. They're not my norm, but I've got an important meeting, and..." Emma let her excuses fade. Damn, but the man smelled good. It took all the will she had not to suck in a deep breath or start licking him from head to toe. Before she did something even more embarrassing, she somehow found the strength to pull out of his arms, though the absence of his touch felt like a pang deep inside her chest. "Thanks. I should be fine."

The elevator chimed and came to a stop, the doors sliding open. "This is me. Stay vertical." He was off with a wave, leaving her to finally breathe easy once more, though her heart had yet to slow its fevered racing.

She was still feeling rattled and off-kilter when the elevator reached the twelfth floor. The doors slid open and she quickly realized why there wasn't a suite number. It turned out that Ryker Investments occupied the whole floor. She told herself not to get angry or annoyed with the fact that this company, that already had so much, was trying to wipe her dream off the face of the earth.

Trying not to wobble, she made her way to the front desk, ignoring the look she got from the receptionist as she gave her name. Nancy, according to the name tag on the desk, tapped on her keyboard and then gave Emma a smile. "He'll be with you momentarily."

Emma took a seat on the plush, but all too modern, sofa and waited. And waited. She should be at her restaurant getting ready for the night's service, instead of sitting there waiting to be graced with Ryker's presence. And to top it all off, she'd nearly killed herself trying not to be late.

A handsome man in a well-fitting tailored suit showed up. Finally. Was this Ryker? Or just another one of his henchmen? She cursed herself for not taking a minute to look up the guy on the Internet. Time was just so damned tight. "Ms. Sparrow? If you could follow me?"

He showed her down a hall, opening the door to a large corner office, and then closing it behind her, leaving her stunned by the wall of glass and the amazing view. High up as they were, she could see all of Portmore and the ocean just beyond. A million-dollar view if ever there was one.

She took a wobbly step towards the chairs, her nerves completely on edge—until she saw the man behind the desk. *Crap.*

"Sweetheart—or should I say Ms. Sparrow?—I'm glad to see you've managed not only to remain upright, but more surprisingly, are uninjured. Have a seat." Quinn Ryker...the man from the elevator...except that he'd tossed away the façade of the sexy biker. Though the stubble and just-fucked hair were still in play, he was now in a meticulously tailored business suit that probably cost him more than her month's rent—and he still looked damn good, curse him. "What can I help you with today?"

Emma plopped herself unceremoniously in a chair, trying not to curse and feeling like a complete fool after the elevator incident. He'd probably had a good laugh, knowing exactly who she was the entire time. And damn, but he'd left her rattled. She'd gone over what she'd wanted to say to him a million times, rehearsed it in her head, knowing that there was way too much riding on this. And now? She couldn't think of anything but cursing the bastard to hell.

Reaching into her purse, she pulled out the letter his company had sent her and thrust it at him. "You know full well why I'm here."

Ugh...so much for trying to win him over to her side with niceties and logical arguments.

"You own the Old Port Bistro." Quinn stood and walked around his massive mahogany desk, leaning against it and casually stretching out his long legs in front of him as if he didn't have a care in the world. He loomed over her as she sat in the chair, only increasing the feeling that he had the upper hand. "I've been there on several occasions. You make a damn good steak. Consider me a fan."

"So then why the hell aren't you renewing my lease? We're doing well; we've gotten great reviews. I've never been late with the rent. I just don't get it." She wanted to scream with frustration. Wanted to reach over, wrap her fingers around his neck, and throttle him until he turned blue.

"It has nothing to do with your restaurant." He shrugged as if none of it had any consequence. "I purchased the building about six months ago with a certain plan in mind, and unfortunately for you, my project requires the building in its entirety."

"Just like that, huh? Easy peasy." Her jaw was clenched so tight she was going to need dental work. "So, what about my restaurant? What about my employees and the people who depend on that

income? You can't just tell us to move, damn it. It cost a small fortune to design and build that space—and we had a renewal clause
in our lease."

He shrugged with a sigh. "I'm afraid the lease you signed had a
renewal clause that was only valid with the original owner. Once the
owner sold me the building, the renewal clause no longer applied,
though it did require that I honor the lease to term. Which I've
done. Now, if there's nothing else, I'm afraid I have other matters
requiring my attention."

How could she have been so stupid? At the time, she hadn't
been able to afford the costly legal fees, and thought her lease was a
standard agreement. Yet the contract had been so convoluted with
legalese, she had no doubt they'd been able to slip in a clause that
escaped her.

Emma felt as though she might be ill. Her face felt numb and
her ears were ringing, as if all the blood had drained to her lower
extremities. She wasn't one for hysterics, but her entire life was on
the line. And more—*so much more.*

She refused to let him dismiss her as if none of it mattered.
Because it did matter, more than anything. Her eyes stung with
threatening tears as her life teetered on the edge of disaster. "What
the hell am I supposed to do? I can't afford to move my restaurant.
It took a fortune to make it happen the first time around—every
penny I had. And we're established in that location now. We'd lose
half our clientele if we were forced to move."

With her restaurant situated in the historic port district of
Portmore, a large ocean-front town in northern Massachusetts, a
good portion of her business came from the tourists who stayed in
the nearby hotels, in addition to the local businesses. Even if she
could scrape together the money to build at a new location, there
was a good chance the whole thing would never get off the ground.
And it had taken her years of working her ass off to get that money,
climbing up the ladder in a field dominated by men who wouldn't
take her seriously until she forced them to see the error of their ways.

"It's nothing personal, Ms. Sparrow. Just business." He crossed his muscular arms in front of his chest as his gaze settled on her with a curiosity she hadn't expected to see.

She shifted in her seat, and bit back the tirade she wanted to unleash on him. "It's not just business, Mr. Ryker. And to me, it's damn personal. It's everything. My career, my savings, my life." Crap. There was a lump forming in her throat, though she refused to show any weakness by shedding tears.

His brow furrowed and his eyes darkened as he took her in, his lips twisting and pressing together as if in contemplation. "I'm not an unreasonable man. Perhaps…we can work something out."

Relief washed over her, and she nearly jumped out of her seat to hug him. "*Anything.* I'll do anything to make this work."

Amusement slipped into his openly triumphant smile. "I'm glad to hear it, Ms. Sparrow."

2

QUINN KNEW ALL ABOUT EMMA Sparrow and her restaurant. He'd purchased the building six months ago and had every intention of overhauling it into a larger project. But what he hadn't told her was that he'd wanted her from the moment he first laid eyes on her a few months ago when he'd walked into her restaurant to grab some dinner.

She'd been standing there in the open kitchen that allowed diners a view, rattling off orders to her staff like some five-star general in complete command of her armies. The food had been incredible—yet unpretentious. Just like her. And he'd been desperate for more—her included—from the very first bite.

He'd frequented her establishment more times than he'd liked to admit, taking clients and friends there, all as an excuse to see her once more. In a world he found increasingly boring, she'd offered him a bit of entertainment and beauty—and he could easily watch her work for hours and never tire of it.

However, today was the first time he'd ever spoken to her, touched her. And damn, but he was already in deep where Emma was concerned. He had to have her. Even if it was just for one night, to get her out of his system.

He had no time for a woman in his life, short of satisfying his healthy sex drive. Yet for Emma? He'd happily carve some time out of his busy schedule if it meant getting her naked body under his. And he was damn near willing to do anything it took to get those fuckable lips wrapped around his cock.

She was certainly pretty, but in an effortless and unconventional way: her mahogany hair pulled back into a messy ponytail with long shaggy bangs, big hazel eyes, and her berry-red lips in a pout that made him want to make good use of that mouth of hers. As for the rest of her, she might be petite, but the girl still had curves— *real curves*, in *all* the right places. She was a natural beauty, and *all* woman. *Nothing* like the women he normally dated—which may very well be a good thing, since more and more, he found himself bored and uninterested with them.

They were gorgeous and smart but they were always too willing to please with the expectation that they'd be rewarded with extravagant gifts and luxurious trips. And that was fine—it was an unspoken agreement that gave them what they wanted, and allowed him some sexual release without having to give it much thought. Yet he found himself just going through the motions.

Emma? Well…she didn't exactly seem the sort to happily go along with anything he wanted. That much was evident from the way she ran her kitchen and chefs. And damn, but that was a total turn-on. He liked that sort of challenge, liked the hunt—and liked the capture even more.

Though she'd likely tell him to go fuck himself under normal circumstances, he now had something she desperately wanted. He felt like a bit of an ass to use her predicament to his advantage, but he'd already given her more thought than he'd given any other woman, and he certainly wouldn't be losing sleep over his tactics if it landed her in his bed. Anything to scratch that itch and get her out of his system, so he could get on with his life.

Because he did want her. Even more so now that he'd had the chance to meet her, to touch her, to feel her sexy body and lush curves pressed against him until his cock swelled with a need that demanded satiation. She was feisty and determined, smart and strong-willed. His perfect match.

And he would have her. Of that, he had no doubt.

He knew what it was like to start from nothing, to work his ass off for every penny. The odds had always been against him, but he'd made it work out of sheer stubbornness and determination. He saw that same fight in Emma, and it made him want her all the more.

She wasn't one who waited around and expected someone to give her everything on a silver platter, as if she deserved it for simply being pretty. That was evident in the way she ran her restaurant. She fought for what she wanted and worked damn hard for it. He had to admire that. And maybe he'd cut her a break that would also work to his advantage.

While running his hand across his rough stubble, in no hurry to shave anytime soon, he gave it some thought. There was still time to make changes to the plans he had for the building, seeing that they weren't set to meet with their other investors to finalize the deal for another month. The building was already his, and though the investors would eventually get a say, that wasn't until they'd all signed on the dotted line.

It might mean shifting some things around, or even losing an investor or two, but he was more than willing to do it, if it meant he got his way with Emma. It's not like he needed their money anyway. "I'll tell you what…I'll see if I can incorporate your restaurant into my current plans for the building. It wasn't what I originally had in mind, but you've piqued my curiosity, Ms. Sparrow, and…I find you intriguing."

"Do you, now?" Her gaze narrowed, as if trying to figure him out. "And why would that be?"

He shrugged, knowing he had the upper hand. "Emma Sparrow. Full academic scholarship to the Culinary Institute. Graduated with highest honors. Spent a year at Le Cordon Bleu in France, before working your way to head chef by age twenty-five, while at some of the finest restaurants across the country, and finally opening your own place at the age of twenty-seven. *Quite impressive.*"

He'd caught her off guard, her eyes going wide as she shifted in her chair. She clearly wasn't one who was used to praise, even if her accomplishments were notable. "So, does this mean you'll extend my lease?"

The fire in her eyes, the determination…he imagined she'd be amazing in bed, and his cock reacted predictably. "Yes—but in exchange, I want us to get to know each other better. I've got several functions I need to attend, and I want you…on my arm and by my side." *And in my bed, under me, around me, any way I can have you, sweetheart.* "I'll also need you to accompany me on my trips overseas."

Emma's eyes went wide as she balked. "*Me?* No offense, but did you forget what I'm like in heels? You should let me keep my restaurant just for saying no to you, since I'm sparing you from becoming the laughingstock of your colleagues. Trust me on this one. I'm not the girl you want as your date."

He gave her a casual shrug, not wanting her to know the sort of effect she was having on him. "I'm sure you'll somehow manage, and since you *are* the girl I want in my bed, I'll happily overlook a stumble or two, especially when I'll be the one who'll be there to catch you."

Her eyes went wide and her jaw dropped open. "*Wait*…you think I'm going to *sleep with you?* To keep my restaurant? *Have you lost your mind?*"

"It's a simple matter, Ms. Sparrow. These functions usually bore me to tears, and you'll do a fine job of keeping me entertained. As for the finer details of our arrangement, I don't think it'll take long for you to come around." He'd yet to meet a woman who could resist him for long, and yet he found it curious that, with Emma, it felt like nothing more than bravado on his part—and damn if that wasn't a rare position to find himself in.

She shook her head as a furious blush swept across her cheeks and the swell of her breasts, making his cock go even harder in response. "There's *no way* I'm sleeping with you."

"You say that now, sweetheart. But if it makes you feel better, then very well...we can table that for now, and revisit that clause in our agreement at a later time." She'd come around—he'd make damn sure of it.

"What if I already have a boyfriend? Did you think of that?" She cocked her head as if she'd suddenly won the argument—which she hadn't.

"Ms. Sparrow, I saw the way you looked at me in the elevator, and if you do have a boyfriend, he clearly doesn't mean much to you. Since you seem the sort to be loyal to the guys you date, and knowing the type of schedule chefs normally keep, I'm going to assume that there's no one waiting for you to get home, and no one who'll be upset by the fact that I'm going to fuck you until you can't walk a straight line—when you're ready, of course." And damn if he wasn't looking forward to that day—a day he was determined to make sure was damn soon.

"You're insane." Her eyes blazed with fury, but all he could do is think of how he'd put all that heat to some damn good use. Repeatedly. And every which way he could think of.

"I know what I like—and I know what I want. You can't fault me for it." It was how he lived his life. Everything he had, everything he'd built, was because he decided what he wanted, and then worked his ass off to make it happen.

"No...I'm sorry, but there's *no way* I can do this. I've spent a *lifetime* trying to be taken seriously in a male-dominated world. Do you know what it's like to get male chefs to give you any professional respect as a woman in the kitchen when you want to be more than a prep cook?" Her small but capable hands clenched into fists, color flaming her cheeks. "I refuse to have you turn me into some...*object*. It's *not* happening."

"Well, if your pride's more important than your restaurant, I guess this conversation is over." He sat back in his chair and picked up some contracts he needed to review. "You can see yourself out, Ms. Sparrow."

He wasn't trying to be an ass, but after years of negotiations, he knew how to get what he wanted. And he wanted her.

Emma got to her feet, though he didn't bother looking up from what he was reading, knowing that she'd yet to leave and was no doubt debating her next move and coming up empty. He finally set aside the paper with an exaggerated sigh. "Was there anything else, Ms. Sparrow?"

Her jaw was clenched tight, but she was looking less stubborn about marching out of his office and sacrificing her restaurant. That said something about her too—that she was smart enough to know what was on the line. "I want some time to think about your offer."

"Do you, now? I didn't realize the offer was still on the table." He leaned back in his chair with the slightest of grins, tenting his fingers in front of him as he took her in. Before today, he'd only ever seen her from a distance, but she certainly was something to look at, especially when her temper was up. He could only imagine what she'd be like in bed, full of passion, so responsive...Quinn couldn't wait.

"Isn't it?" She cocked her head and pinned him with a steely glare. "Because I somehow doubt you're done toying with me. Or are you going to tell me I'm mistaken?"

He shrugged. "I'll tell you what...you have twenty-four hours to give me your answer. If you have any questions regarding the arrangement, you can call me directly." Pulling out a business card, he jotted down his personal cell phone number—something he rarely gave out—and held it out to her. "Have a good day, Ms. Sparrow."

She swiped the card from between his fingers and stuffed it in her back pocket with a shake of her head, her ponytail bobbing as she spun on her heels, nearly wiped out, and then marched to the door, swinging that fine ass of hers.

This was going to be more fun than any one man deserved.

3

E MMA RATTLED OFF THE LIST of ordered items. "Last ticket of the night. Come on, guys…let's push this through. Finish strong." Emma was exhausted, but it felt good, especially since staying busy helped burn through her anger from dealing with Ryker and distracted her from all her problems.

One by one, the plates were placed in front of her at the pass for her final approval and finishing touches. Once she was happy with the results, she gave her waitstaff the okay to take the dishes out to the diners. She turned back to her crew, four in total, since they were still missing Tony. "Nice job tonight, especially since we were still down a man."

She leaned against the counter to give herself a minute before the day's events invaded her mind, escaping from where she'd locked them away, so she could focus on her job. What Ryker was asking of her was insane. And it didn't make any sense. Why the hell would he bother to even give her a second look when he could have any woman in the world?

Jake slipped in by her side, his height making her feel even smaller than her five-two frame normally did. And damn but his looming height did nothing but remind her of Quinn Ryker and the way his hard muscular body had felt as he held onto her during that elevator ride. "Are you all right? You've been distracted since you left this morning, and you've yet to say how the meeting went."

She hadn't had a chance to really talk to Jake, since things had been so crazy by the time she'd finally gotten back to work. And what would she say anyway? That she was contemplating prostituting herself to save the restaurant and their jobs? Quinn may not have been upfront about that part of their bargain, but she knew it was implied.

Worse still, she'd likely do whatever it took to keep the restaurant going since without it, she'd never be able to afford the costly physical therapy her brother needed. Nate had been hit by a drunk driver, who'd been uninsured and driving with a suspended license. With the case still in the courts, and little luck they'd get any compensation from the driver, her brother was forced to pay the hospital bills himself.

Nate had health insurance, but with another party responsible for the accident, his insurance only covered a portion of his bills, and even then that only paid for the most basic therapies, rather than the ones that he most benefited from. Still…he was lucky to be alive after such a horrific accident, and the last thing she wanted was to bail on him when his options were already so few.

"Honestly? I don't know what the hell I'm going to do. He gave me twenty-four hours to think over his offer, which means that by tomorrow morning, I better have some sort of answer for him." She let out a weary sigh, and debated drowning her troubles in the chocolate mousse cake they'd had on the menu for the night.

"Well, what is there to think about? If it'll save the restaurant…" Jake shifted to look at her—really look at her—his brow furrowed as he analyzed her weary face. "What were his terms? Is he increasing the rent?"

"If only it were that simple." She debated keeping the terms from Jake, knowing just how protective he could be of her. "He's asking for a slightly…different…arrangement. Not one I'm sure I'm ready to accept."

Jake's chocolate brown eyes narrowed as he leaned in just a hair, as if trying to read her mind. "What sort of arrangement, Em? You're not saying…"

"Kind of." She shrugged, suddenly feeling exhausted. "I don't know, Jake. He said he wants me to accompany him to functions and business trips as his date."

His jaw clenched, and he looked ready to punch something. "And he expects you to sleep with him."

"Probably, though I told him that wasn't part of the deal—and he agreed." Would he honor their arrangement, though, if she didn't sleep with him?

She didn't know Ryker or the type of man he was, though she could probably guess. Billions in the bank, used to getting his way, women falling at his feet… And frankly, after the way her body had reacted to him on the elevator, being in close proximity to him would leave her in far too vulnerable a position.

"Do you actually believe he won't try to sleep with you? Because I don't, Em. And if he hurts you, I'm liable to murder the bastard." She didn't doubt it for a second. Jake was her best friend, and had always stood by her side.

"He wouldn't hurt me. At least I'm pretty sure about that. He's a well-known businessman, and he wouldn't take that sort of risk. But I don't get what the hell he's up to. I'm not exactly the supermodel type guys like him normally date." That was an understatement when she stood all of five two.

"Those other women don't hold a candle to you, Em." He gave his head a shake. "It'd be one thing if you just needed money—I'd happily loan you what you need, but there's nothing I can do about him renewing the lease. So…I hate to ask, but what are you going to do?"

"I wish I knew."

⤳——⬦⬥⬦——⤵

After a night of restless sleep, Emma awoke feeling groggy, miserable, and no closer to figuring out whether or not she was going to accept Quinn's offer. Never in a million years would she have thought the answer to that sort of proposition would be anything but an emphatic *go fuck yourself.*

She'd busted her ass getting people in her field to take her seriously, to gain their respect and be treated as an equal. To be looked at as a chef—period—her gender of no consequence. She'd worked hard to get to that point, toiling in restaurants all over the country as she perfected her skills. And now she was debating whether or not she should be arm candy for a billionaire who could have whatever the hell he wanted and who was holding her restaurant hostage.

She didn't bother with the heels this time. Nor with the pretty blouse. If he wanted her, then there'd be no pretenses, no facades. He'd get the real deal—who she really was. Not some fantasy.

After yet another lukewarm and dismally short shower, Emma towel dried her hair, threw on a pair of worn and comfy jeans, and a baggy oversized sweater with a pair of shearling boots. It was October in New England, which meant there was a chill in the air, especially when the wind came whipping in off the ocean. She grabbed her jacket and car keys, and headed out of her building, only to find Quinn waiting for her, straddling a motorcycle—something classic-looking, though it was clearly new, decked out in shiny chrome and metallic black paint.

Her cheeks flushed hot as she cursed under her breath, suddenly feeling completely flustered to find him on her doorstep, especially when she still didn't know what she was going to do about his proposition. "What the hell are you doing here?"

"I'm taking you for a ride up the coast so we can discuss our arrangement." He had one helmet resting in front of him and another behind him, presumably where he expected her to sit, clinging to him for dear life.

Well, he could think again—even if she couldn't get the image of her body pressed against his out of her mind. She needed to focus, especially with someone like Quinn, since she doubted he missed a thing. And she needed to hold onto her anger.

"You still haven't answered my question. Why are you here? And how the hell did you get my home address?" Not that it would be all that difficult to find the information. But that wasn't the point.

He flicked his eyebrows up at her teasingly, no doubt fully aware of just how good-looking a man he was. "Don't go getting your knickers in a twist, Emma. May I call you Emma?" Not that he waited for her answer before continuing. "All your personal information is on the lease to your restaurant. Or did you forget that I'm your landlord?"

"How could I possibly forget when you're blackmailing me? Isn't that illegal or something? And this meeting was supposed to be at your office, not on the sidewalk outside my apartment." She'd been hoping to decide whether or not to say yes to his proposition during the drive over to his office. Now, she was out of time and still clueless as to what she'd tell him.

With a shrug and a smile that made her stomach quiver—a smile she was sure was a regular in his arsenal when it came to getting his way with the ladies—he held the helmet out to her. "Here. Change of plans."

"Well, I'm not getting on that deathtrap, so you can guess again." No way. Not after she'd seen the damage of a bad accident first-hand—and her brother had been in a car, surrounded by steel and airbags and safety features. Not simply whizzing around with nothing but a helmet on his noggin for protection.

He looked over her shoulder to her apartment building, jutting out his chin to motion to it. "So, this is where you live? Looks like a lot of the older details are still intact."

"Yeah…like the ancient furnace, drafty windows, and nonexistent hot water." She was tired of standing there on the sidewalk, but there was little chance she'd be climbing onto his lap—*bike.* Climbing onto his *bike!* She tried not to groan. Her crazy schedule didn't exactly leave a whole lot of time for dating—or all the other fun stuff that came with it. And Quinn might be an ass, but every nerve in her body felt like it had come alive since running into him. Which only made her guard go up. "Are we going to have that meeting or not?"

His eyes narrowed just a little, as if taking her in and analyzing her for weak spots in her armor. "We can head up to your place, if you'd prefer. Or are you going to let me take you for a ride? I promise you'll enjoy yourself, darling."

There was no way she was letting him into her place. It was the size of a mouse hole, and though she made the small space work with a loft bed and by utilizing every square inch, including the vertical spaces, there was no way it was the place to conduct a business meeting. Not to mention, the thought of her alone with him in that small space...she didn't trust her body—or him—to behave.

"Hop on, Emma. You're out of options, and I want to go for a ride. Burn off some energy." He held out the helmet to her as she cursed under her breath, her heart galloping. He must have seen it, too. "Don't look so worried. I'll take it slow—and you have my word, I won't let anything happen to you. You're safe with me."

She couldn't believe she was going to do this. Of all the asinine things.

His sultry smile kicked up as she grabbed the helmet and climbed onto the bike behind him. Adrenaline already had her blood pumping frantically through her veins, as she shifted in her seat, her body pressing against his.

Quinn looked over his shoulder at her with a disarming smile and got ready to put on his helmet. "Just get your helmet on and then hold onto me nice and tight."

She did as he asked while the bike roared to life beneath her with a low reverberating rumble that worked its way to her very core. Before she knew it, they were off as she clung to Quinn for dear life, her arms wrapped snugly around his muscular torso.

True to his word, he kept his speed slow as they rode down to the port and then along the ocean. By the time they were outside of Portmore, she was still clinging to Quinn's impressive form, though she finally managed to relax enough to get back some of her senses—her surroundings, the wind whipping around them—and the feel of Quinn's body against hers and the effect he was having on her.

The hard vibrations of the bike as she straddled the seat certainly weren't helping matters, and it was nearly impossible to not want to climb into Quinn's lap, her throbbing clit aching for release, and her nipples hard against his broad back. It'd be a miracle if she didn't come the moment he looked at her with one of those sultry smiles of his, though being so turned on had, at the very least, distracted her from her fears and worries.

Quinn didn't take them too far out of town, finally pulling over by a rocky bluff that overlooked a sea sparkling in the sunlight. With their helmets off, he reached around and gave her a hand off the bike, as if anticipating that her legs would be shaky. If only he knew the truth of it. "Easy there. Don't want you hurting yourself."

Still holding onto her hand, he slipped off the bike and pulled her into his arms, holding her tightly against him as he brushed her cheek with the back of his fingers. His touch was warm and his proximity had her sucking in a breath as she tried to ignore the effect he had on her body—a body that was already riding a razor's edge. Between his height and muscular build, he felt like a force of nature, impossible to ignore.

"That wasn't so bad, now, was it?" With his scent filling her head, it took all she had to focus on his question, and the reason she was there. She wanted to be angry with him, wanted to push him away, but having him so close after that cursed bike ride was causing her synapses to misfire.

"It's fine until there's an accident and someone gets their head cracked open." Or ended up so mangled, they'd never be able to fully recover.

His green eyes darkened and his jaw tightened. "I wouldn't let anything happen to you, Emma. Ever. You're safe with me. I hope you know that."

Suddenly, he felt too close and with her emotions riding just below the surface, she needed some space, some air that didn't carry his masculine scent, and she needed to remember that he was holding her restaurant hostage. "You're not the only one on the road, Ryker."

"Call me Quinn." When she tried to pull free of his embrace, he let her go, though she didn't get far before he grabbed her hand and twined his fingers with hers. "Come on."

She wanted to ask him where they were going, wanted to tell him that she needed to get to work, that she didn't have time for walks on the beach. Instead, she let him lead the way over some rocky outcroppings, the smell of the salty sea and the cries of the gulls overhead soothing her rough edges. As busy as things were with work, she didn't get to the beach as often as she'd like. Pity, too, since it was one of the reasons she'd moved to Portmore.

Quinn kept a firm hold of her hand, lending her the support she needed to make it over the rocks when her footing was unsure. Letting go of her for just a moment, he dropped down to a lower ledge with the graceful movement of an athlete, before turning to grab her by the waist and lower her down as if she weighed nothing. Her body brushed against his, and she once again found herself in his arms, an ominous reminder of what he was asking of her.

"You're gorgeous, you know." His smile went from hot to smoldering as he brushed the hair from her eyes, his touch electric so it took all she had not to lean into him. She wanted to curse him to hell—even as she fought the urge to sink her fingers in his thick, dark hair and pull him to her for a mind-blowing, knee-wobbling, heart-pounding kiss.

What the hell was wrong with her?

Ever since the moment she ran into him at the elevator, he'd had an effect on her like no man before. But he knew full well what he was doing to her, and was taking complete advantage of her weaknesses.

"Look, the beach is lovely, but I have to get to work, so if we could get around to discussing the reason for this meeting, I'd appreciate it." She tried to pull out of his arms, but he held her firmly to him, making it difficult for her to think straight. "You're holding onto me…"

"So I am." Those green eyes of his lit up with a fire that had her sucking in a breath as she attempted to ignore the ache of need between her legs. "Have you made your decision then?"

Now that she finally had to give him her answer, she felt like she might be ill. Because that decision she'd been debating? Well...there was really only one option, as much as she hated to admit it. There was too much on the line, too many people depending on her, and she'd been backed into a corner.

This time, when she tried to pull free of his strong arms, he let her go. Ignoring the sudden lump in her throat and the burning in her eyes, she wondered how the hell she'd ever gotten herself in such a messed-up situation. "I'll agree to your proposition."

"I'm glad to hear it, Emma." His brow furrowed a little as his intelligent eyes took her in, making her want to look away from their intensity, even as she forced herself to hold his gaze. "Don't look so worried, love. I swear, I'll think of ways to keep you entertained."

Perfect. "I don't need to be entertained, Quinn. I just want to make sure my restaurant's safe. And until I know that's the case, there's no way I'll be able to do anything but go through the motions."

"Then I'll just have to try extra hard." He grabbed her hand and led her down off the rocks and onto the sandy beach.

"I'm not going to sleep with you, Quinn. It's not happening." She couldn't—even if he looked like a sex god. He was dangerous—in so many ways—and the root of her current problems. Their little agreement might give him a whole lot of leeway, but it was the one thing she'd taken off the table and she had to hold onto that.

She refused to become one of his playthings, though why he was even bothering with her when he could have his pick of the most beautiful women in the world, she didn't know. Nothing about her stood out—she was too short, too curvy, and her thick hair had a mind all of its own if she didn't tie it back.

"Keep telling yourself that and maybe you'll actually start to believe it. Because from where I stand? You want me just as much as I want you." He tossed her a sideways glance with a smile that made her blush and sent a shiver of need through her very core.

She forced them to a stop and spun to look at him, feeling the full power of his presence. If she had any hope of maintaining her distance, she'd have to do a better job of pushing him away and setting some boundaries—something she seemed to have a hard time doing when it came to him. "Are you going to be a pain in the ass every time I have to deal with you? Because if you are, then I might have to reconsider my answer."

In a lightning-quick move, she found herself pinned to his muscular body with a strong arm wrapped around her waist, as she cursed under her breath, her struggles futile. He brushed the hair from her face, his touch lingering against her skin.

"You're a feisty little thing, aren't you?" He slipped his fingers through her long hair and fisted it, pulling her head back so she'd be forced to look at him. Despite all her thoughts to keep him at arm's length and not let him have an effect on her, she was finding it impossible. Her breathing was coming in shallow gasps as her nipples went hard against his chest and her clit throbbed double-time, threatening to push her over the edge and leave her coming then and there, with him having barely laid a finger on her. She couldn't help her body's reaction to him taking control, even as her mind protested it. "I bet it'd be a whole lot of fun seeing whether or not you can be tamed."

Quinn lowered his head, bit her bottom lip and then, as her lips parted in surprise, covered her mouth in a forceful kiss, his tongue thrusting against hers as he tightened his grip. Unable to escape, her body gave up its fight and succumbed to the fire he'd stoked in her, softening against his muscular form.

He deepened their kiss so she felt it down to her very core, his hands running up her waist to cup her breasts, teasing her nipples so she felt a corresponding tug between her legs. When a needy whimper escaped her lips, he swallowed it, claimed it as his, leaving her unable to think clearly. Her brain told her to run, but her body had other ideas, her tongue clashing with his as she fisted her hands in his shirt, and her hips shifted against his long hard cock, desperate to feel him fill her, stretch her so tight, he'd have her coming with a single thrust.

This was what happened when one neglected one's sex life.

He broke their kiss, but showed her little mercy as he pulled her head back, biting her neck and pinching her nipples, the sharp flicker of pain mingling with pleasure and making her wet, as she ached for him to take her. *Curse him.*

Nuzzling her, his lips wandered to her ear, his hot breath on her skin contrasting with the cool ocean air, sending a shiver over her skin as she clung to him. "See, sweetheart? You want me just as much as I want you. You want me to fuck you and make you come, over and over and over again, until you don't even remember your name...until the only name on your lips is mine."

She swallowed the moan that wanted to escape. Desperate to keep him from seeing the truth of just how bad she wanted him, she somehow found the strength to pull away from him. He was merciful enough to let her slip free of his hold, though he still held her hand, twining his fingers with hers. No doubt, some sort of cat-and-mouse game.

With a bit more distance between them, the foggy haze in her head started to clear so she could think straight, though it left her wondering what the hell she was doing and how she could let him have such an effect on her. "Just take me home, Quinn. Please. You got your answer—and you've gotten what you want. I've agreed to your proposition."

"Maybe, though I don't understand why you're fighting me so hard on this. It's clear you'd enjoy yourself. I'd make damn sure of it, sweetheart."

"It still doesn't mean I'm going to sleep with you. That's not part of our deal." She'd get through this. She had to. It was a simple trade— one that did *not* involve sex. She'd be going out to dinners and parties. And yet she was already having one hell of a time keeping her distance. She wanted to stay angry with him, but every time he touched her, he weakened her resolve and she succumbed to his charms.

"It may not be part of our deal, but it doesn't change the fact that you want me as much as I want you—even if you insist that you don't." He brushed her hair from her face as the wind caught it, her eyes slipping shut as he touched her cheek, his fingers just a little rough as if he'd been working with his hands, despite his billions.

Emma forced herself to shift away from him, to try to break the spell he was casting, his mere presence intoxicating. Once again, she reminded herself what was at stake. She needed to keep a clear head. "What I want doesn't matter, Quinn. I just want to save my restaurant."

"And I just want to fuck you. It's a win-win situation." The way he spoke those words…as if it were a simple matter of no consequence and she was already his. It left her with a frisson of awareness and excitement coursing through her body.

Shaking her head clear, Emma let out a frustrated sigh. "I'm not some sort of prude, but…bloody hell...What is it with you? Do you even bother to get to know the people you sleep with?"

He shrugged. "If that's what it takes to make you feel comfortable, that's fine by me, darling. Ask away. I'm happy to answer whatever questions you have if it means we can stop talking this to death. I want you, Emma, and I'm not known for my patience, though I'll do what it takes if it means you'll stop pushing me away and let me get you in my bed. I have plans for that curvy little body of yours and the sooner we can get horizontal and naked, the better."

"This isn't a game of fifty questions, Quinn." She threw her arms up in frustration, and would have started to pace if he hadn't grabbed her hand. "Haven't you ever had a normal relationship where things just take their course instead of it being negotiated like some sort of business transaction?"

His eyebrow perked up in annoyance as she got the full brunt of his gaze. "I've got a busy schedule, and frankly, I haven't found anyone worth taking the time to get to know further." His gaze then softened. "Until now, Emma. If you need to be courted and seduced, if you need time to get to know me, then I'll do it. But just so we're clear—when all is said and done, *I will have you.*"

She had to laugh. Never before had she ever met anyone quite like him. So cocksure and arrogant. And yet…somehow, he made it work. "You sound awfully sure of yourself, Quinn—and we haven't even gone on our first date."

"I've never been more sure of anything in all my life." He pulled her into his arms and held her to him, making it impossible for her to ignore his hard cock as it pressed against her inquiringly. And damn, but it pushed her back to that edge as she felt herself go wet again, even if her mind told her to stop being a horny fool. "As for our first date, that'll be tomorrow night. A gallery showing in town. Nothing too fancy, though I'd like you to supplement your wardrobe with whatever you'd like. I'll have a credit card dropped off for you this afternoon to take care of whatever expenses you might incur."

"Tomorrow? I can't, Quinn. I need to be at my restaurant." This arrangement of his would never work. What the hell was she thinking? That every event would just so happen to fall on her night off? "I'm sorry, but I need more of a heads-up so I can schedule my staff accordingly."

"I'm sure you'll figure something out, though if you'd like, I can send someone to cover you for the night." The smile that tugged at his lips was infuriating, and this time when she shrugged free of him to pace, he let her.

"You don't get it, do you? I'm not running a goddamned hotdog stand. Old Port's considered one of the best restaurants in town, and I can't risk its reputation." Not when she'd busted her butt to make sure every customer had an amazing experience.

"Sweetheart…I'm not some amateur." His green eyes sparkled with mischief, and damn if it didn't make him even better-looking than he already was. *Bastard.* "Would Finn Scott do?"

Her jaw dropped open in shock, no doubt making her look like a stupid fool. "Finn Scott? *The* Finn Scott?" She couldn't believe it. He was one of the most innovative cooks in the area, and had won countless awards and accolades, despite being only a few years older than her. "But…*how*…and why the hell would he agree to work at my restaurant?"

"Because he's one of my oldest friends and he owes me a favor or two. Besides, he's in the middle of renovating his current restaurant, and is antsy to get back into the kitchen."

Touché. The man was good. She had to give him that.

⚬────⚬⚬⚬⚬────⚬

Emma spent the following morning trying on one outfit after another, under the keen scrutiny of Ivy Winston's gaze. Her fashionable neighbor and sweet friend had agreed to go shopping with her, though it didn't make the day any easier to stomach. This was so far outside Emma's norm and comfort zone, it acted as a constant reminder that she was essentially picking out outfits to be a billionaire's arm candy and plaything.

Ivy must have returned with another armful of clothes, though all Emma could see was a pair of pink patent leather heels pacing below the doors of the dressing room. "If you're going to a gallery opening, you'll want to look elegant but not too formal. Do you need help with the zipper?"

"No...I've got it. Sort of." Emma wanted to groan as she shifted the fabric of the dress around, feeling like she'd been put in a straightjacket. The fit was far too snug for her curves, especially compared to what she was used to wearing, and though it looked okay, she'd go crazy if she had to stay in that dress for any length of time. "If he wants elegant, then I'm afraid he's better off finding himself a different date."

"Sweetie, we'll have you looking like you just stepped off the Paris runway by the time we're done." Clearly, Ivy was delusional.

Exasperated with trying to make the dress comfortable, she gave up and pulled the dressing room door open. "This is *not* going to work."

Ivy's eyes went wide and she clasped her hands together. "Oh! You look gorgeous, Emmie. That shade is stunning against your skin, and the way it hugs your curves... He's going to drop dead when he sees you. I still can't believe you're going out with *Quinn Ryker*. Most women would sign their souls over to the devil for a date with him."

"Well, they can have him." She tugged at the dress, already desperate to get it off—not a good thing if she planned to keep Quinn from sleeping with her. "The deep raspberry color is really nice, but the fabric has no give, and I'll lose it if I have to be in this sausage casing all night long." She'd spend the night holding her breath, yanking on the hem, and wanting to murder Quinn for making her go through this nonsense, all so she could keep her restaurant. It was absurd.

"Got it. You definitely need to be comfortable, and though this shows off your gorgeous figure and would definitely be a showstopper, there's no point to any of it if you can't enjoy yourself. And we definitely want you to enjoy yourself." Ivy waggled her eyebrows at her with a mischievous grin before tackling the pile of clothes she'd already gathered. She pulled another dress from the pile and handed it to Emma, before flicking her long red hair over her shoulder. "Try this one. It's nearly the same color, but the fabric is luxurious, and it has plenty of stretch, so it'll accentuate your curves, but still be comfortable."

Emma locked herself in the dressing room and attempted to get out of the dress she was wearing so she could try on the next one.

Ivy's voice sounded through the door, thrumming with excitement. "Once we've got the dress picked out, we'll grab lingerie and then find a pair of heels to match."

"I can't do heels, Ivy. I'll kill myself." It was going to be a total disaster.

"Not by the time I'm done with you, sweetie. And don't forget, I also booked us in at the spa. You won't recognize yourself by the time we're done."

Now that wouldn't be a stretch, since Emma barely recognized the person she'd already become.

4

HAVING REFUSED TO MEET EMMA at the gallery, despite her insistence, Quinn climbed the stairs to the second floor, taking note of the nonexistent security in her apartment building. With no lock on the main entry door, anyone could come up the stairs and either break into her apartment or be lying in wait for her, hiding in the shadows of the stairwell, since the lone sixty-watt bulb was doing little to fight back the darkness.

He didn't like it. Not one bit. Something would need to be done.

Was that the reason she hadn't wanted him to pick her up? He'd first wondered if it was because she didn't want him in her personal space, given the circumstances of their arrangement. But now he had to wonder if it was because of the apartment itself, given the age of the building and its problems. Probably a little of both, though he could fix at least one of those issues.

He'd have to give it a bit more thought, because there was no way in hell he could leave her to live in a place that didn't have basic accommodations like hot water—and he sure as hell wouldn't let her risk her safety. Portmore was a safe enough community, but with the steady flow of tourists, there were always strangers wandering the streets, especially once the bars let out. The thought of her being injured…attacked…left him with a ball of rage spiraling in his gut.

She must have heard him coming up the creaky steps, because she was slipping out of her apartment and locking her door, before he'd even had the chance to knock.

And damn, but he practically did a double take. The girl was *gorgeous*.

Emma was wearing her dark brown hair down in a loose tumble of thick waves, and the raspberry-colored dress she wore hugged every curve like a lover's touch. His cock went hard and strained against the fabric of his pants, making him want to drag her back into her apartment and forget the gallery.

Though he'd seen her plenty of times while she'd been working, she looked like a completely different woman tonight. There was a tender vulnerability in her that he hadn't expected to see, and he couldn't help but feel protective of her.

"We should go." She was already heading down the stairs, leaving him to follow.

When he caught up with her on the sidewalk, he was determined to keep her from racing through the evening in an attempt to avoid him and distance herself.

Stepping to her side, he leaned in and kissed her, brushing his lips against hers as he rested a hand on her hip, his fingers splaying possessively over her curves, the fabric silky soft to the touch. She wasn't overdressed, nor was she too casual—a perfect match to the sport coat and shirt he'd paired with dark jeans. "You look lovely."

Even in the dim light of the evening, he could see a blush creep across her cheeks, her body stiff under his touch. "Thanks. I'm glad it meets with your approval."

It was impossible to ignore the sarcasm in her voice, no doubt a reminder that the only reason she was there was because of their agreement. She was strong-willed and proud, but he was just as guilty of those faults and couldn't hold them against her. Even though he secretly wanted to hold her close and fill her head with whispers of sweet words, there was another part of him that was happy to play her games.

"My approval's earned, sweetheart, though you're well on your way." Quinn linked his hand with hers, surprised when she didn't pull away or tell him to go fuck himself.

"And it'll be a cold day in hell when I need your approval for anything." She gave him a sweet smile that made him want to fuck her then and there.

"You may not need my approval, but I guarantee you, that before long, you'll want it." He brought her hand to his lips and kissed it sweetly, though he held her gaze with a look that told her he'd have her before long. Because damn...he couldn't remember ever being so taken with someone—nor had he ever been more determined.

"You can't truly think that'll ever happen." She glared at him with such an incredulous look, he couldn't help but laugh.

"Maybe not, but you're so fucking sexy when you get angry, that I can't help but misbehave—and you do make me want to misbehave, Emma, in *so* many ways." He brushed her cheek, her skin hot to the touch. "Look at you blush. If I had to hazard a guess, I'd bet it's because, deep down, it turns you on to know that I'm going to have my way with you. And though you'll probably try to deny that you enjoy fucking me, your body will betray you. We'll both know the truth...that no other man has ever given you such pleasure."

She looked at him so sweetly, batting her eyelashes at him as her voice dripped with honey. *"Bite me,* Quinn."

"Happily, sweetheart." He couldn't help but laugh as he offered her his arm, wondering just how long she'd last before she slapped him. "Shall we go?"

"You make it sound as though I have a choice." She gave him a sarcastic smile, before replacing it with a no-nonsense look as she climbed into his car—a vintage Aston Martin he'd taken out of storage just for the occasion. "Anything I should know going into this? I wouldn't want to embarrass you or screw up some business deal you've been working months to land."

"No, not really. It's a charity event that I've contributed to, rather than business. Just try not to look like you want to carve out my liver and we should be fine."

The artwork was provocative, with black and white photos of nudes, and yet he found his gaze constantly wandering back to Emma, his hard-on yet to let up. They chatted with the gallery owner and the other guests, but his focus never drifted for long. And he wasn't the only one who'd noticed her.

Nearly every guy in the place had checked her out at one point or another, their eyes all but undressing her, and though he had no claim on her, he was damned if he could control his jealous streak—a streak that had never before reared its ugly head. There was something about her that made him want to drag her off to a dark corner and fuck her senseless, to mark her as his own. Claim her as his. And he found that damn curious, since normally, he didn't care enough to bother getting worked up over any of the women he'd dated, barely sparing them a second thought.

With an arm around her waist, he pulled her close and lowered his head to her ear, picking up on the spicy notes of the perfume she wore. "Do you see how every man in the place can't help but look at you? Do you see how much they want you? But they can't have you, darling, because you're mine—*all mine.*"

The thought of another man's hands on her made him want to hike her dress up and take her, pinned against the glass wall of the gallery with everyone watching as he staked his claim, so they'd know she was his—his and no one else's. His own little art installation.

"Well, they can look all they want. It makes no difference, since there's only one reason I'm here, Quinn, and that's because you require it of me in order to save my restaurant." Emma hadn't pulled away from him, so when she spoke, her breath danced over his skin, the heat of it sending an ache of need to his groin.

Ever since he'd laid eyes on her that first time in her restaurant, he hadn't been able to keep her from invading his thoughts, his constant hard-on an inescapable reminder of how much he wanted her—a hard-on that refused to stay away, no matter how many times he'd jerked off to his few memories of her. There was no way she should have this sort of effect on him, and now that he had her in his arms, he knew there was no going back.

"You may be here because of your restaurant, but I plan to make sure you enjoy yourself." Still keeping her close, he steered them towards the back of the gallery, hoping there'd be fewer people there. "I want this to be a mutually enjoyable and beneficial arrangement for both of us."

She stopped and spun to face him, fury in those pretty hazel eyes of hers and a blush across her cheeks and chest, making him wonder what it would be like to taste her skin, to taste her very essence. "You've essentially blackmailed me into being here by holding the lease on my restaurant hostage, and now you're worried that I'm not enjoying myself?"

"I guess it's the gentleman in me. And I do hope you took full advantage of the line of credit on the card I sent and bought some sexy little bits of lace to go under that dress." He knew he was playing a dangerous game since she already hated him, and yet he couldn't resist seeing her get flustered. The way her chest rose and fell in her anger accentuated her perfectly firm curves, and made his cock strain against his dark jeans, eager to have her.

She shook her head as if to clear it, and he'd have sworn that if they hadn't been in a room full of people, she'd have decked him. "Have you lost your mind?"

"Maybe I have, since I can think of little else but getting you naked." Still holding onto her hand, he spun her into his arms like a skilled dancer, so that her back rested against his chest and his cock pressed against her ass. Unable to resist, he nuzzled her, running his lips over the warm skin of her neck.

She surprised him when she leaned back against him with a needy exhale. He couldn't help but tighten his hold on her and rake his teeth over the slope of her shoulder, desperate to elicit more of a response from her. She gasped as her hips tilted back against his cock and he let his arm slip around her waist to pull her even tighter to him as he nipped and kissed her delicate skin, unable to resist doing so.

"What the hell do you think you're doing?" Her words were a quiet hiss and he knew he was playing a dangerous game.

When he spoke, his breath was warm against her ear, eliciting a shiver from her body, still pressed against him. "If I had to hazard a guess, I'd say I'm making your nipples go hard against the soft fabric of your dress, and I'm making your panties wet. And if I thought you'd let me, I'd turn you around and kiss those *oh-so-fuckable* red lips of yours until your knees buckle."

Then, before she had a chance to respond, he somehow found the strength to pull away from her, twining his fingers with hers as he led them to the next work of art. She resisted for a moment but then followed along with a glare that made him smile.

"Are you always so forward with women you've only just met?" She tried to extricate her hand from his, but he pulled her to him and slipped an arm possessively around her waist.

"They don't normally interest me the way you do—and they certainly don't make me try this hard." He cupped her cheek and loosened his hold on her, wondering if she'd pull away. She didn't. And damn if that didn't make his heart race. He didn't know what it was about her, but he seemed drawn to her, desperate to have her, and especially after that kiss on the beach, he didn't think anyone else would do until he fucked her out of his system.

"But why are you even remotely interested? I know the type of women you date, and I'm nothing like them." She shook her head with a huff.

"You're right—you're nothing like them. You're exquisite—and somehow, I don't think you have any idea just how captivating you are." And she was. Intelligent hazel eyes, pouty full lips, high cheekbones, a thick mane of hair that made him want to fist it, and amazing legs that led up to curves that didn't quit. Every man in the place knew just how special she was—though he'd made sure that they also knew he'd staked his claim, and not one of them was brave enough to challenge him.

"I don't get you." Her brow furrowed as if she were deep in thought, trying to figure him out. "I can't decide if you're a bastard or if it's all an act."

He brushed his thumb over her lips, taking her in with a hungry gaze, though her words still lingered in the air between them. "What's your gut telling you?"

Her eyebrows perked up as her eyes shifted towards a smoky green. "My gut? My gut's telling me to run."

"Are you sure it's not telling you to kiss me? Like this…" Nuzzling her, his stubble rough against her smooth skin, he captured her mouth in a kiss, gentle yet forceful, his tongue dancing over hers as his fingers tangled in her hair. His cock ached with anticipation as he deepened their kiss, loving the way her body leaned into him as her lush curves pressed against his hardened length.

Somehow, he managed to bring their kiss to an end, though he was damned if he'd be able to stay away for long, every fiber of his being desperate to claim her as his, to possess her until her lips could speak nothing but his name, and her body could do nothing but ache for his touch. When he finally managed it, his breathing was still heavy, his words but a whisper in her ear. "Maybe it's telling you to throw caution to the wind and come home with me."

"That's not part of our deal." All night long, she'd reminded him that she was only there because of their arrangement. Well, he'd make sure that changed before the night was through. He'd have her wanting him, just as much as he wanted her.

His fingers splayed over her hipbone as he pulled her to him, catching the elusive scent of her perfume. "You're right. It's not part of our deal, though there's nothing to stop us from enjoying ourselves. I want you, Emma. And when I want something, I'll do whatever it takes to get my hands on it."

"You see?" She gave him a smug smile. "Just like that, you're back to being a bastard."

With a shake of his head, he couldn't help but laugh. "I'm a bastard because I find you attractive?"

"No. You're a bastard because you think you can just take whatever you want. Just like that."

Momentary anger flared in his chest. He wasn't some spoilt little rich kid who grew up getting everything he wanted. In fact, it was the complete opposite. He'd had to claw his way to the top from that cramped and dingy apartment in Southie where he'd shared a bedroom with his two brothers. He'd been determined and had worked his ass off to get what he wanted, and when he had become successful, he'd done his damnedest to do right by the people around him and his community.

"That's where you'd be mistaken—not that you care to find out the truth when you can cling to your fantasy of me being an evil bastard." He wanted to pace, wanted to shake her until she came to her senses, wanted to kiss her until she could no longer push him away. His tone cooled noticeably. "Come on then. Might as well get you home. I'm sure you wouldn't want to have to share the same air with such a bastard any longer than necessary."

"Quinn…" She grabbed his hand when he started to walk away from her. "I'm sorry—I really am. I was out of line, and it's not as though I didn't kiss you back."

He pinned her with a steely stare, though she didn't look away. "Tell me, Emma. Do you actually mean any of that or are you only saying it because you're worried about your restaurant?"

She let out a sigh and gave him a shrug. "If anything, I probably lashed out *because* I am so worried about my restaurant. Believe it or not, I'm not usually such a bitch."

With his anger dissipating in the face of her honesty, he couldn't resist teasing her, a smile upon his lips as he took her in. "Are you sure? Because you look like you're pretty adept at busting people's balls."

"Maybe just a little." And damn if that wasn't the first genuine smile he'd gotten out of her since their elevator incident.

He took a risk and brushed her cheek, his pulse racing as he touched her. "Come on then. Let's get out of here. Are you hungry?"

"Starving."

5

"WHERE ARE WE GOING?" EMMA couldn't quite figure Quinn out. He seemed to be every bit the playboy bachelor his reputation made him out to be—right down to the fancy sports car—and yet, there was another part of him that seemed completely different from the brash and cocky jerk he'd built his tabloid reputation on. Every time she got ready to murder Quinn for being such a pushy ass, the sexy, helpful guy she'd first met in the elevator would show up to make her question her judgment.

She looked over at him as he maneuvered the sleek sports car along the coastline. He was handsome in a way few men were, somehow managing to look rugged yet refined, mixing bad boy with billionaire bachelor. Dark hair that looked like he'd been running his hands through it, a stubbled jaw, eyes so green and intelligent, and a mouth that was completely kissable. It was a dangerous combination that left her far too vulnerable.

And damn, but the man knew how to kiss. Toe-curling, heart-pounding, *drag-me-to-your-bed* kisses that left her wanting to forget that she was mad at him for threatening her livelihood. It made her want to find out what else that mouth was capable of—and that was a huge problem. She couldn't lose sight of what was at stake. There was too much on the line to let herself get lost in a fantasy. That wasn't her world—nor would it ever be. And she'd worked too damn hard to let it all go to hell just because she couldn't remember the last time she got laid.

"There's a little place I like to go to. Just hope it'll be up to your standards, Chef." He gave her a sideways glance and a smile that reached his eyes and lit them from within.

"I like it when you call me that." Though why she was telling him, she hadn't a clue. At the very least, it reminded her of why she was there. Because when he was being nice? It was so easy to forget he was the enemy.

"Sweetheart...I'm happy to call you whatever you'd like as long as it's my name on your lips when you come." Damn if his words didn't leave her at once furious and completely turned on, if she were being honest with herself.

"What is it with you? Why do you always have to go there?" She shook her head and shifted in her seat, though it did nothing but increase the heavy ache between her legs.

"I know what I like—and I know what I want." He gave her a casual shrug as he pulled down a side road that continued to run along the ocean. "You can't fault me for being honest with you. And I don't lie, sweetheart—nor do I beat around the bush. Life's too short."

There was a pain in his voice that caught her off guard, though it left her wondering if she'd imagined it. His gaze was focused on the road ahead of them, his eyes dark in the dim light of the night.

"Well, I do appreciate the honesty." It was something at least—and a big something at that, especially after finding her last boyfriend in bed with the barista from the café they'd frequented. "I've been lied to in the past by someone I trusted, and I can't stand it. It makes me question everything that's said to me, and I end up feeling like a fool afterwards for being stupid and naïve enough to believe the lies."

"If anyone was a fool, it was the person who lied to you. I have no tolerance for lies and deceptions. I'm just sorry you had to go through that." Quinn's brow furrowed, and though his eyes were still on the road, his gaze was intense as he glanced over at her for just a moment and cupped her face. The fact that he'd gotten so angry on her behalf caught her off guard, especially when they barely knew each other. And when he reached over and twined his fingers with hers before bringing her hand to his lips, the gesture at once sexy and old-fashioned, she couldn't help but like him just a little more.

She found it hard to ignore the way his touch made her feel, especially when he was being sweet. Squirming in her seat to ease some of the aching need he was eliciting in her traitorous body, she tried to remind herself that she was only on this date to save her restaurant. And it had nothing to do with his touch or his kisses.

She forced herself to focus, especially since it'd be too easy to let him get her worked up like he had on the beach. And who knew what she'd be liable to do if he got her all hot and bothered again. "I'm sure everyone's been ruthlessly lied to at some point in their life. I can't be the only one, right?"

"No… It's unfortunate that it happens as often it does." Quinn glanced in her direction, giving her hand a squeeze, his touch strong and warm. "That's one thing I promise you, Emma. I'll always be honest with you."

"I appreciate it—and I'll certainly do the same." Emma wasn't sure why, but it meant a lot that he'd given her that small token of respect. And once more, it had her wondering who the real Quinn Ryker was.

He maneuvered the car into the parking lot of an old-style greasy spoon, the wheels crunching on the crushed gravel. "I know it's not much to look at, especially now that it's dark out, but there's a great view of the ocean, and the burgers can't be beat." He cupped the back of her neck and pulled her in for a quick kiss, and though she hesitated just a moment, she'd be damned if it didn't leave her wanting more. "Come on, sweetheart. I'm starving."

In more ways than one, no doubt.

While she tried to clear her head, he came around the car and got her door, offering her his hand to help her out of her seat. With her gaze on him, she felt her dress shift up her thighs, Quinn's smile widening in response as she no doubt showed him a long expanse of leg and probably accidentally flashed him too, the way her night was going.

"You've got great legs, sweetheart." He pulled her to her feet, her body brushing against his as he held her close and nuzzled her, his hands slipping to her waist and gripping her firmly. She felt caught, captured, and she swore the shiver of need that pulsed through her body made her feel more alive than she had in a very long time.

"Thanks." Crap…he had her blushing like some school girl.

He was so tall, so muscular, and his grip was so strong. He overwhelmed her senses and left her desperate for more.

What the hell was she doing?

Enemy Number One—straight ahead. *Focus.* But with his clean, manly scent filling her head, all she could manage was a ragged breath as she leaned in towards him. He pressed her up against the side of his car, making it impossible to ignore his hard length. His lips found hers in a kiss that stoked her need for him and had her fisting his shirt in her hands, barely resisting the urge to wrap her legs around his waist.

Damn him to hell.

She wanted to protest, but when he nipped at her neck, all she could manage was to roll her head to the side to give him easier access, and instead of curses, a needy moan escaped her lips. Just as she was getting ready to reach down and stroke him, he took her mouth in a sweetly lingering kiss, before pulling away, leaving her body reeling.

"Come on, kitten. There'll be plenty of time for that later." He knotted his fingers with hers and pulled her close to his body, possession in the gesture, though he disarmed her with a light kiss to her temple. Even as Emma's brain told her she was playing right into the trap he'd set for her, her heart softened, yielding to the way he made her feel. "I'm starving and need to be fed."

That must've been the understatement of the year, because the man finished off his double patty burger, all his onion rings, a handful of her fries, his strawberry shake, and was now looking for dessert. "So tell me, Lois, what would you recommend to finish up our meal?"

Their waitress, an older woman in her sixties, gave him a sly smile, their relationship clearly a familiar one, from what Emma had seen. "I don't know why you insist on asking each and every time, when you always order the same exact thing."

"Never know...the menu might suddenly change." Quinn gave her a shoulder shrug and a smile that made him look far less like the ruthless and shrewd businessman she'd seen at work. "I suppose we'll go with the usual then. And if you could bring two forks, I'd appreciate it."

Lois leaned towards her as she turned to go. "Honey, you must be pretty special if he's sharing his cheesecake with you."

Emma managed a smile as Lois walked away, though curiosity got the better of her. "Do you come here often with your dates?"

He shook his head, looking rather serious. "Never. You're the first."

That didn't make any sense. "So...why me?"

"Tell me—what did you think of your burger?" He sat back in the booth and crossed his arms in front of his chest so that the fabric of his shirt pulled tight, accentuating all those rock-hard muscles underneath.

That was an easy enough question to answer, given her profession. "It was fantastic—juicy with a nice crust from the hot flattop grill. Just the right amount of fat. The potato bun held up well to the weight of the patty but was still soft and didn't distract from the flavors of the meat—which was perfectly seasoned, by the way. Classic condiments, and the homemade ketchup was a very nice touch, especially with the little kick of cayenne and smoky paprika."

His lips curled up into a sexy smile as his green eyes sparkled— and damn if it didn't make her breath catch. "*That's* why I've never brought any of my other dates here. I knew you'd appreciate this place for what it was. Most of the women I've dated only care that a restaurant is trendy, expensive, and there are plenty of other people there so they'll be seen with me and, with luck, make it into a tabloid or society paper. Beyond that, as long as there's plenty of champagne, the food could be crap, and they'd never notice—or care for that matter, since they don't tend to eat more than a few bites."

She shook her head, trying to clear it. "I don't get it. You don't exactly sound thrilled with them, so why date that sort of woman?"

He shrugged. "It's been easy. Convenient. I'm usually too busy to give any of it much thought or effort. And they've been happy."

"So you get your needs met without having to try too hard. Right?" *Clearly.* Though it didn't shock her, she was surprised to find that it did actually bother her.

"I'm not denying it, but…" He sighed before leaning forward just a little, closing the distance between them so she could see the flecks of blue and gold in his green eyes. "More and more I find those sorts of dates tedious. Hell, even the sex feels repetitive and uninspired—and it's pretty bad when you can't even get much enjoyment from getting laid."

"Is that why I'm here? Because you're bored with the women you normally date and want an inspired lay? Lovely." It was impossible to keep the sarcasm from her voice.

"Why shouldn't I want more? I've worked damn hard to establish myself and my business." He ran a rough hand across his jaw and gave her a smile that had her breath catching and an ache starting up between her legs. "I can finally take a bit more time to focus on things other than work—and I like you. A lot. So if you have a problem with that—outside of the fact that you're only here because of your restaurant—then I want to know where the hell you're getting hung up so we can fix it."

"It's not that easy, Quinn." What was he thinking?

"Why not? We're already halfway there, since you'll be joining me for whatever events I have planned for the foreseeable future."

He reached over and twined his fingers with hers. "I'm just asking for a little more."

"You mean, you're asking for what I explicitly said was off the table." It figured. She knew it'd all come down to this.

"Say it." He ran a lazy circle over the back of her hand with his thumb.

"Fine. Sex. You want to fuck me." Her face flushed, though whether it was with anger, excitement, or desire, she wasn't quite sure. Maybe it was all three.

His gaze took her in, his lips curling into a half-smile that reminded her of a wolf that had its prey cornered. "Would you like that? And please, sweetheart, let's not start telling each other lies. I like this relationship too much for untruths."

"Relationship?" She scoffed and shook her head. "Usually those don't involve blackmail."

Though his gaze was stern, humor tugged at his lips with an easy smile. "Answer me, Emma. Would you like me to fuck you? And remember that you've promised me honesty."

With her pulse racing and her breathing shallow, she couldn't believe he'd maneuvered her into such a position. Damn him.

She took a deep breath and somehow found the strength to look him in the eyes as she answered, though she'd be damned if she could keep her voice from sounding shallow and breathy. "Even if I did, I don't just act on every whim. It's far more complicated than that."

Emma stopped talking when Lois put a slice of the most delicious-looking strawberry cheesecake on the table between them with a smile. "Two forks for the lovebirds. Enjoy."

Quinn looked up at Lois with a smile, not looking the least bit annoyed about her lovebirds comment. "Thanks, Lois." Once she was gone, he shifted his gaze back to Emma. "It doesn't have to be complicated, Emma. I like you, and I think you like me at least a little. Even then, you don't need to like me in order to enjoy sex. You just need to want me—and you do want me. I'd put money on it. So, tell me, darling...tell me that you want me to fuck you...that you want me to make you come so hard that your legs give out and you can't do anything but scream my name."

She let out an annoyed huff, not quite believing they were having this conversation. "Why do you insist on going there? Just eat your damn cheesecake."

"The cheesecake's fantastic, but that's not really what I'm interested in eating, love." He gave her a crooked grin as his eyebrows flicked up and he fed himself a forkful of cheesecake, his tongue peeking out to lick at his lips.

She wanted to groan. Wanted to slip her hands between her legs and find some relief. And she wanted to reach across the table and slap him for doing this to her. Frankly, she'd had enough. "Fuck off, Quinn."

He burst out laughing. "I love how feisty you are. Love that you want me so badly, and yet you hold your ground. So, keep fighting me, darling, because that'll only make my victory all the sweeter when I finally have you. And I will have you, Emma. Every way imaginable. Would you like that, my sweet dirty girl?"

"The only one here with a dirty mind is *you*." Desperately needing a way to distract herself lest he see that her mind had already gone to all the places he'd been describing, she took a bite of cheesecake and nearly had an orgasm then and there. "*Wow*...that's really good." She wanted to hate everything about him, and yet he was making it infuriatingly hard for her.

"It's different, isn't it?" He took another forkful, and she followed suit, forgetting to be angry with him as she let the flavors play over her tongue.

"It doesn't have the normal cream cheese flavor, nor is it grainy in texture like ricotta. If I had to guess, I'd say mascarpone." And instead of a graham cracker crust, they'd used a butter cookie crust and then topped it all off with freshly macerated strawberries.

"Couldn't tell you, love. I just like eating it—and I like watching you eat it too, with those plump red lips of yours. I bet they taste so good right about now." He leaned forward with his arms propped on the table, and damn, but he looked ready to devour her.

Tired of him teasing her, she figured she could give as good as she got. Swiping her finger through the dollop of whipped cream, she slowly sucked it off her finger suggestively, holding his gaze and reveling in the fact that his eyes had darkened, and he'd bitten his bottom lip. "They're even sweeter now—not that you'll get to taste them."

"Like hell I won't."

6

QUINN DIDN'T HESITATE TO TAKE advantage of Emma's flirting. Reaching across the table, he cupped the back of her neck with a firm hand and kissed her, ignoring her protests and the fact that there were other customers watching. Her lips parted as his tongue found hers in a kiss that left him wanting to sprawl her across the table and finally have a real taste of her.

When he somehow managed to break their kiss, he could barely control his need for her, his breathing heavy as he spoke. "So fucking sweet, and so sexy. Just like I knew they'd be."

He dug out his wallet and tossed far too much money on the table, as he always did, knowing Lois's income was meager. However, the last thing he'd been expecting was for Emma to grab her wallet, as if expecting to pay for her dinner. "Don't you dare, Emma. Dinner's on me. Always. Put your money away." And though he'd never in a million years let her pay, there was something in him that appreciated the gesture, especially when none of the other women he'd been with would have ever thought to offer.

She growled in frustration, but stuffed her wallet back in her bag. "I don't want your money, Quinn."

He pulled himself out of the booth, and gave her a hand getting to her feet. She slid out of her seat, showing him a long expanse of leg as the hem of her dress rode up her thighs. It was impossible to keep his erection from straining against his jeans, and in the position she was in with his crotch at her eye level, there was no hiding the effect she was having on him.

Her wide eyes drifted from his cock up to his face, before turning into a glare after being caught ogling his hard-on. "Quit looking at my legs. It's bad enough I had to put on this dress and heels."

"At least you've managed to remain upright. Your abilities seem… greatly improved. And sweetheart, I'll most certainly look at your legs if you're looking at my cock."

"You're just so funny." She shot him a look over her shoulder as she moved towards the door, and he swore she was the sexiest thing he'd seen in a very long time, all attitude and sass, and clearly not aware of just how gorgeous she was. "As for walking in these things, you can thank my friend Ivy for that. She insisted I practice and wouldn't let up until I could manage it without killing myself."

"Then I'll have to send her my thanks, since I prefer you in one piece." They stepped out into the cool night air and the salty scent of the ocean. Though it was October, the weather had been unusually mild, even if the evenings had started to cool down. "Don't suppose I could interest you in a walk on the beach? I'm not ready for this night to come to an end just yet."

"I'm here on your dime, Quinn." The bitterness in her voice caught him off guard—and she must have realized exactly how it sounded because she turned towards him and grabbed his hand. "Wait…I'm sorry. That was unfair and mean of me to say."

"It's not far from the truth though, is it?" And why the hell did it bother him? It's not as though he hadn't been the one to set it all up—and the women he normally dated were far worse and far more blatant about what they wanted from him, even as they lied about it.

"Actually it is." She let out a sigh as she shook her head, as if she were tired of fighting with him. "It's just that I've never been the sort to ask anyone for help. If something needs to get done, I do it.

So the fact that something as important as the fate of my restaurant is completely out of my control makes me crazy. And yes...I'll do whatever it takes to keep the Old Port going, since there's too much at stake. But being blackmailed into being your date or sleeping with you puts my back up and makes me feel exactly like the women who date you just because they want something."

"And that's all because I've forced your hand." When she nodded and looked away, on the verge of tears, he felt a pang of remorse that he'd made a critical mistake with her. He knew she was different—hell, it'd been the reason he liked her so much—and yet he'd expected her to react in exactly the same way as all the other women he'd been trying to avoid. "Come here, Emma."

She shook her head and turned away from him, though he refused to let her go, especially when she was clearly upset. With an insistent touch, he took her hand and pulled her to him, relieved when she didn't fight him. He held her tightly to him as she leaned her head against his chest and wrapped her arms around his waist, letting out a deep breath, some of the tension in her body easing. "I know you think I'm a bastard and it's probably not far from the truth, but I'm sorry if I've put you in an uncomfortable situation. That was never my intention."

She pulled away just enough to look up at him and then went up onto her toes to kiss his cheek. "I appreciate you saying so."

"Come on. Let's go for that walk on the beach. I'm not ready to take you home yet." He brushed the hair from her face as a breeze tugged at her locks, though it was no more than an excuse to touch her skin and continue holding her close. With her lush curves still pressed against him, his body couldn't help but react to having her so close, and that meant he was left struggling to put a coherent thought together that didn't involve her naked with his cock buried deep inside her.

"As long as I get to kick off these heels—and as long as you promise to behave yourself." He was already leading her towards the beach, the path visible just beyond the parking lot.

"Emma, I don't make promises I can't keep." And there was no way he'd be able to keep his hands off her for long. "I refuse to lie to you, and I'll admit, I'm still hoping the night will end with you screaming my name as you come apart in my arms."

She gave him a teasing glare, her full lips pursed as if in thought. "I'm starting to think you say that sort of thing just to get me all riled up."

"Think what you want, kitten. But we both know that if we were to throw away all pretenses, you'd find that you not only like me, but you want me. Just as bad as I want you. Admit it." He knew he was being arrogant, but he didn't care when he knew it to be the truth.

"There's no point in continuing to tell you that you're a bastard. Who even talks like that?" She shook her head as he laughed, though when she tried to pull free of him with a halfhearted attempt, he refused to let her go.

As soon as they got off the wooden boardwalk and onto the sand, Emma stepped out of her heels while holding onto him for balance, reminding him of their elevator escapade. She tossed her shoes onto the boardwalk but now that Quinn had her in his arms, there was no way he was letting go of her so easily. Not when he'd so desperately wanted her all these months.

With her curves pressed to his body, he lost what little control he'd been managing to hold onto. He caught her bottom lip between his teeth as he palmed her ass and pulled her to him, his hard-on throbbing with a dull ache against his jeans, insisting on a bit of release.

"Sweetheart, I want you, and I'm not going to rest until I have you."

"You said this wasn't part of the deal, Quinn." And yet she wasn't pushing him away, but rather leaning into him.

"It's not." He trailed kisses down her throat and to her ear, until she was all but moaning in his arms.

"*Damn you, Quinn.*" Emma fisted her hands in his shirt and kissed him, her tongue finding his with a needy whimper, her hips shifting and pressing against his cock. And when she spoke, it was with her lips still pressed against his, as if she couldn't quite pull herself away. "I don't want to like you. Especially not like this."

He couldn't help but smile as he trailed kisses down her neck, sucking, nipping, loving how her body responded to him, her little moans of need and pleasure. "Why fight it when I can give you pleasure like you've never felt before? Don't you want my cock filling you, stretching you tight, making you come so many times you won't be able to keep count?" As if her silence was permission enough, Quinn cupped her breasts, his thumbs making devastating passes against her nipples.

Emma made a strangled sound, kissing him hard as she gave in to her body's demands, and gripped his cock through his jeans, stroking it as it pulsed in her hand. Quinn swore he'd come right then if she kept it up, like some teenager touched for the first time, and he couldn't remember ever wanting anyone more than he wanted her.

Yet this wasn't about him. It was all about her. About her needs. Her pleasure. It had to be. And he'd be damned if he knew when that epic shift had happened. He always made sure he took good care of his dates, but it'd still been all about him and his satisfaction. With Emma? It felt different. Completely. Which was definitely uncharted territory for him.

He spun her around in his arms, so her back pressed against his chest as his hands slipped up to her breasts, cupping the weight of them before pinching her nipples. Her back arched to press her breasts more fully into his palms, even as she let out a needy sound of protest. "Hush, sweetheart…I promise to take good care of you."

"You don't know how long it's been." Emma shifted in his arms, rubbing her plump ass against his hard cock, and making it difficult for him to resist taking her right there with her on her hands and knees, fucking her as she pushed back to meet his thrusts.

He caught the edge of her dress and slipped it up her thighs, nice and slow, the silky fabric shifting to expose her pearly skin as it caught what little light had made its way to the beach. Unerringly, his hand found the lace front of her panties, cupping her, applying just enough pressure over the thin fabric to elicit another moan from her. With his lips at her ear, he let his words dance over her skin.

"Tell me, Emma... Tell me that you want me to touch you. That you want me to fuck you with my fingers until you quiver and come." Her head dropped back onto his shoulder as he nipped at the delicate skin of her neck, where her pulse raced just below the surface. "Say it."

He could feel her struggle with it, and yet in the end, she still spoke the words he wanted to hear. "I want you to make me come, Quinn. Please..."

"Such a polite little thing. So proper and obedient, and yet so fucking sexy." Holding her to him with a firm arm across her chest, he cupped her breast and pinched her nipple, as his other hand pushed the lace of her panties aside and he slipped his fingers against her slick folds. "Oh, sweetheart...you're already so wet. All those times you told me that you didn't want me... Such a naughty girl for telling lies when you promised me honesty. I think you might need to be punished..."

"*Bastard...*" And yet her hips tilted towards his hand, clearly wanting more.

Impatiently, he grabbed at the delicate lace and tore it free of her body, loving the gasp that escaped her lips. Now free to easily explore, he dipped two fingers in past her slick opening as his thumb circled and pressed her clit, teasing her as he started to fuck her with his fingers. She was so responsive, like liquid heat in his hands. "You're so tight...and so ready... Do you like that, kitten? And please, be honest with me, seeing as the evidence is literally at hand. Your silky wetness...all for me."

"Fuck...*Yes.*" When he started to pick up the pace, curling his fingers inside her with each thrust, she let out a needy whimper as if struggling to get the words out. "More, Quinn...I'm so close. Harder..."

Pinching her nipple, he bit her neck and slipped a third finger into her—and just like that, her body tightened around him. She cried out and quivered in his arms as her orgasm tore through her in an intense release, his name on her lips.

Still holding her to him, he pulled his fingers free of her and brought them to his lips, his tongue flicking out to taste her. "You taste so sweet, Emma. Next time I'm going to have you properly. I'm going to spread you out on my dining room table and make a meal of you."

She spun in his arms and fisted her fingers in his hair, dragging him to her and kissing him, her mouth hard on hers as her tongue clashed with his. His cock ached for release and wild as she was, there was little chance Quinn would be able to resist her for long.

Yet he managed to bring their kisses to an end, though he hadn't a clue as to how the hell he pulled that one off. And as much as he wanted her, he knew it was what he had to do. "It's time I brought you home."

"Why?" She shook her head, her brow furrowed in confusion as she started to pull away from him. "What the hell, Quinn? You can't just make me come like that and then take me home minutes later."

He held onto her a moment more, not ready to let her go just yet. "I can and I will, sweetheart. This arrangement of ours is on my terms."

"How could I possibly forget?"

7

E MMA DIDN'T KNOW WHAT HAD gotten into her last night, but
after her date with Quinn, two things were clear: the man
was dangerous and she could not be trusted to act rationally
around him. She'd expected him to be an arrogant and cocky bastard and he'd been just that. But worse still was that he'd been damn
sexy—enough to leave her incapable of denying him. The way she'd
reacted to having him close had totally blindsided her. He may have
been far sweeter and more considerate than she'd expected, but it
still didn't warrant letting him get her off.

"You haven't said much, Em, and you're looking miserable and
distracted. What the hell ended up happening between the two of
you?" Jake was filleting some salmon with a scowl on his face, his
knife-work getting quicker the more annoyed he became. "Do I
need to pay Ryker a visit?"

"No. It's fine. Besides, I don't want to talk about my stupid
date—I want to know how things went here last night with Chef
Scott. How was it? Was he amazing?" She'd probably have gotten
more out of last night if she'd stayed at work. Not that Quinn hadn't

given her a mind-blowing orgasm. She had to give him credit, even if begrudgingly so. The man was damn good with his hands.

"Em…" Jake shook his head with a smile, his scowl long gone at the first mention of Finn Scott's name. "Chef Scott was amazing. I mean, to have him here for dinner service? I wish you'd been here. You'd have really liked him."

"I'm sure I would have. He may end up having to cover for me again—if Quinn has any other events he needs me to attend." After the way things had gone down, she had no doubt Quinn would want to see her again, if only to gloat. He'd said he'd have her screaming out his name as she came in his arms, and she'd done just that. *Damn him.*

Normally she could get a pretty good read on people, but Quinn left her baffled. He just didn't make any sense. He'd flirted, touched, and teased; made her come, even. Yet when she'd tried to reciprocate, he'd put a stop to it.

What she couldn't figure out was *why.*

"You're going out with him again? You can't be serious, Em." With an angry huff, Jake got back to his prep work.

"What am I supposed to do? If you like your job here, then I have no choice but to keep this up until he gets bored of me. And frankly, he's not exactly what you'd expect." Though why the hell she was defending Quinn, she hadn't a clue.

He pinned her with those deep brown eyes of his, so that the flecks of gold stood out, making her want to analyze the color closely. "Then why the hell do you look so miserable?"

She shook her head with a shrug, not quite sure how to answer him.

"Chef?" Emma turned to find Bobby, one of her prep cooks, standing there, his gaze not quite reaching hers as he shifted his weight from one foot to the other. "It's the walk-in fridge—the big one in the basement. Something's wrong with it."

Crap…this was *not* a complication she needed. She quickly washed her hands and her knife, and followed Bobby down the steps into the well-lit basement. She opened the door to the walk-in to find it cool but definitely not as cold as it should be. A quick glance at the thermometer verified her suspicions, and a look at the easy fixes, like the plug and the fuse box, didn't help matters any. "We'll need to transfer all the vegetables to the other walk-in, but the meat..." She cursed under her breath. "We can't take that sort of a chance."

Having been gone yesterday, she didn't know how long the temperature had been off, and couldn't risk anyone getting sick. Luckily, most of the meat was kept in a different walk-in by the kitchen, since it was the most convenient for service, with the basement walk-in housing just the meats that were getting marinated or treated with a dry rub. It was a big loss, but it could have been a hell of a lot worse if it had been her main unit.

With everyone's help, they got the food moved from one fridge to the other, but the repair technician was still several days out. With frustration gnawing at her insides and stress knotting her muscles, she got back to work by Jake's side, trying to make up for lost time.

"Is it just me, or does it feel like we've had shit luck as of late?" It wasn't just the lease, and the walk-in, but all sorts of other issues. Her accounting files had gotten fried, a shelving unit where they kept their bottles of wine had given way, and her fryer completely died. She'd been lucky that she kept a backup of her files online on a secure cloud server, and most of the wine bottles had still been in crates, so they lost only a few, but she ended up having to replace the fryer at a major cost.

"Plenty of shit luck. I hate to say it, Em, but you just can't catch a break as of late." Jake stopped his prep and turned to her with his brow drawn and a pout on his lips. "I know you're going to say no, but you know I have money for the repairs. It's not a problem. Really."

She shook her head no. Emma knew that Jake had inherited a sizeable chunk of money from a great-uncle who'd recently passed away. Probably didn't even need to work, if he didn't want to, yet she didn't feel right asking him for money. It was her responsibility.

"I appreciate it, but I think I'll be okay. I've got a bit stashed in my emergency fund." Not that there'd be anything left in that account if this ended up being a costly repair.

A few hours later, she was nearly ready for service when she spied a familiar form walking towards her. It felt like she had the wind knocked out of her, as she was overcome with a wealth of emotions. "What the hell are you doing here—and who let you back here?"

Quinn's mouth kicked up into a crooked smile, his eyes bright and lit from within. "Such a warm welcome…" He tipped her chin up and kissed her, his lips lingering with unspoken promise. "I'm meeting my brother here for dinner, so I figured I'd check in with you and make sure things were okay between us after last night."

She felt like a jerk for yelling at him, but she could also feel all sorts of eyes watching them—especially Jake's. "I'm sorry, but I can't do this—not now and definitely not here. Things are crazy, and we're getting ready for service. Plus it's already been one hell of a day."

"If I can help in any way…" His brow furrowed with a look of genuine concern, making her think once more that there was a sweet side to him, and perhaps she was mistaken about him.

"Unfortunately, there's nothing you can do. Not unless you have a walk-in fridge strapped to the roof of your car. Mine's decided to die on me." The fridge wasn't even old. Just long enough to be out of warranty. She just had some shitty luck.

He ran a finger down her cheek and gave her a smile. "I can have someone take a look at it—and if not, I can have a new fridge here by tomorrow."

He had to be kidding. "No one's going to come out here on a Friday night to fix my fridge. Not even for you. And I do *not* want you buying me a new one. That's insane—even if I'm grateful for the offer."

He pulled out his phone, swiped his finger across a few screens, and then ignored her when she started to protest the call he was making. She listened to him, so casual, so cool, as he made arrangements to have some poor man drag his butt to her restaurant on a Friday night. Quinn hung up and gave her a smile. "Ryan will be here shortly, sweetheart."

"Thanks." She didn't know what to say or how to feel. "And I really do appreciate it, but…I'm just used to dealing with things on my own. I can't have you rescuing me every time something goes wrong."

"Why the hell not? It's not like it's of any consequence if I buy you a new fridge or help you get your old one fixed. It was just a phone call, Emma. And if I want to help you, I'll do just that. Are we clear?" He raised his eyebrows in question, a challenging look on his face as if daring her to turn this into an issue.

"No, we're not. You may own the building, but I'm still the one in charge of my restaurant. I'm not some charity case—not yours nor anyone else's." She let out a ragged breath and glared at him. "And why do you make me want to argue with you over the smallest thing, when I *do* appreciate your help, Quinn?"

He brushed her cheek, as his eyes darkened and his lips pressed together in a kissable pout that made her want to forget they were being watched. "You're far too stubborn for your own good."

"That may very well be the case, but I don't have time to debate the matter further. I've got to get back to work." Okay…so she was the world's biggest coward. But she couldn't have any sort of conversation with him if it involved him touching her, especially when her staff could see her. She had to maintain professionalism—and work was not the place for this sort of thing.

"I'll be here when you're done for the night." Quinn ran his hand down her arm and linked his hand with hers. "I need to talk to you, Emma, and I won't take no for an answer."

"It'll be way too late. I don't usually get out of here until midnight, and by then I'm going to be tired, cranky, and smell horrible." And she sure as hell wouldn't have the wherewithal to think clearly around him—or resist him for that matter. Last night was evidence of that.

"Midnight it is, then." He leaned in and stole a quick kiss before turning and heading out towards the dining room.

Damn him.

With Quinn sitting in the dining room of her restaurant, Emma started the night feeling distracted, sensing his gaze drift towards her as he watched her work from a distance, their eyes meeting whenever she chanced a glance over at him. And damn but the Ryker boys were hot, the two brothers looking far too much alike with their striking good looks to be anything but family. Yet as they slipped further into dinner service, she no longer had the time to think about Quinn as the orders came in, one table after another.

"What the hell is he still doing out there, Em?" Jake scowled as he glared in Quinn's direction. He'd been in a mood all night. "He can't just sit there."

"He can sit there as long as he likes if he's eating and drinking, and at least the walk-in is getting fixed." She hadn't expected Quinn to hang out as long as he had, but he certainly seemed determined to do just that, and with his brother for company, they at least seemed to be enjoying themselves, no doubt running up a huge tab. That said, if he was expecting her to be bright and chipper after such a busy night, he'd be sorely disappointed. "Let's wrap up this service, yeah? Then we can all get out of here."

Emma had just another few tables to complete, when Ryan, the repair guy, came looking for her. They stepped out of the kitchen and into one of the hall areas near the bar. "I got it up and running, so you should be all set. But…I'm not sure that the issue with the walk-in was due to a defect or wear and tear. Maybe it was an accident and someone didn't want to take the responsibility, but I can't imagine any sort of scenario where you'd accidentally get that kind of damage."

"You mean someone did this on purpose?" The betrayal stung worse than a hundred beestings.

Ryan shrugged. "Look, I can't say that. But if it were me? I'd start wondering who I've pissed off."

Her brow furrowed with worry and confusion. She truly couldn't think of anyone who disliked her enough to do something so malicious, though there was another restaurant just down the road that had not been happy about her opening her doors. The owner was certainly a prick, and there were even rumors he had ties to the mob, but it's not like she gave the guy access to her kitchen. That meant it was one of her employees, which would make perfect sense given the other "accidents" that had occurred. "Thanks for coming out on such short notice. Let me get my checkbook, and I'll wrap you up some food and dessert to go since I no doubt ruined your evening."

She started moving towards her office when he stopped her. "I've already been paid, though I won't say no to a bit of dessert for the old lady. And if you have any other problems, here's my card. Day or night, it doesn't matter. It's never a problem."

Quinn. He must have already paid Ryan so she wouldn't have to. She sent Ryan off with several boxes of food, though she was plagued by the gut-wrenching thought that someone had been malicious enough to cause her problems.

Service was done by the time she got back and clean-up was already underway, though she couldn't help looking around her at all the familiar faces and wonder if someone was harboring some sort of animosity towards her and the restaurant.

With all hands on deck, it didn't take long for them to finish up for the night. She turned to Jake as she unbuttoned her chef's whites, making sure she kept her voice down so they wouldn't be overheard. "The walk-in's all set, though it looks like someone damaged it on purpose."

"Who the hell would do that, Em?" He shook his head, as a scowl darkened his handsome face.

"I don't know, but we need to keep an eye out. And in the meantime, don't say anything. I can't afford to have this escalate." She was exhausted and this bit of news had only drained her further. "I'm going to go. Quinn's been waiting all night."

"That was his choice." Jake leaned against the counter, his muscular arms crossed in front of his chest. "I don't like him, Em. Not one bit."

She wanted to groan, way too tired to have this sort of discussion. "You never like anyone I'm dating."

His eyebrows shot up. "So now you're dating him?"

"No. Yes." Coming in Quinn's arms certainly seemed intimate enough, though she wasn't exactly sure she'd say they were dating. So then, what exactly was she doing? "Ugh, Jake. You're killing me. I'm too tired to think about this and have any of it make sense."

"Well, don't let me stop you from hanging out with your boy-friend." Jake motioned with his chin over her shoulder before turning to go.

"*Jake...*" But he didn't turn around. Just kept going as he shrugged out of his whites and whipped the soiled clothing into the laundry bag.

"Hey... Everything okay?" She turned to find Quinn standing there, scowling in Jake's direction.

"Yeah. It's just been a long night." She glanced over in time to see Jake take off out the back door.

Quinn put an arm around her and pulled her close, and tired as she was, she didn't have the energy to fight him. "So, what the hell's his problem? He better not be giving you a hard time about anything."

"Your clothes are going to stink and get filthy if you keep holding me." She wasn't ready to try to explain her relationship with Jake.

For years, they'd worked together in other restaurants and had become the best of friends. Although she knew Jake wouldn't mind pursuing something more, she just couldn't go there, even if she'd thought about it from time to time. In the end, she always dismissed the idea, not wanting to ruin their friendship.

"I've been thinking about holding you in my arms all night long, so if you think I'm going to let anything stand in my way—especially something that can easily be remedied with a bit of dry cleaning—then you can guess again." He stole a kiss, and though she might soon regret it, she let him. "Are you ready to get out of here?"

"I don't know where you're heading, but I'm going home to boil some water and attempt to take a hot bath." It'd take a bit of fina-gling, and it might not be worth the effort when all was said and done, but she was desperate to soak the day away.

"I think you should come home with me instead." He cupped her cheek and stole another kiss, his touch warm and gentle, reminding her of everything those hands were capable of. "Let me draw you a nice hot bath. I've got a massive soaker tub with massaging jets, and I promise, sweetheart, I'll take really good care of you."

The way he spoke those last words...they held so much promise. Too much. And though his tub sounded amazing, she knew that if she went over there, she'd have a hard time keeping things from getting far more intimate. "Quinn...what the hell are we doing here?"

He nuzzled her, his words drifting over her skin like promises in the wind. "I'm going to take care of you, and you're going to let me. *That's* what we're doing. And I'm not taking no for an answer."

Fifteen minutes later, they were pulling down his driveway. Emma had been sure Quinn lived in some slick penthouse-like condo that overlooked Portmore and the ocean, and could have graced the pages of any modern design magazine.

She was wrong.

Quinn's home did indeed overlook the ocean, but it did so from a rocky bluff outside of town. It was big, but not massive, and the exterior was well lit with accent lights. Emma could only imagine how gorgeous it'd be in the light of day with the ocean view. And yet it was a reminder of just how different their lives were.

He lived in a gorgeous seaside mansion, and she didn't even have proper hot water.

What the hell was she doing?

She then remembered exactly how she'd come to find herself in this predicament. He was holding onto the lease of her restaurant. At least he was far less of a jerk than she'd first thought him to be—even if he still had his moments. "I didn't get to thank you for sending your guy to fix my fridge. I really appreciate it, but...I can't accept your charity. I'm perfectly capable of paying my bills."

"I know you're perfectly capable, but Ryan's on my payroll. I use him to maintain all my properties." He parked in the driveway, turned off the engine to his SUV, and shifted in his seat to face her.

"If you really feel the need to pay me back though, I can think of far more creative ways to call it even."

She shook her head with a small smile, and couldn't help teasing him just a little. "You had your chance last night, Quinn. Should have taken me up on it when I was willing."

"No worries, sweetheart...I'm sure you'll be willing again by the time I'm through with you." Before she had a chance to protest, he was coming around to her side of the car to get her door, a gentlemanly gesture that always caught her off guard these days.

She thanked him, and then followed him into his home, her breath catching not only with the beauty of it, but because there were a whole lot of dogs barreling towards them. "Holy smokes."

Okay...maybe not a lot of dogs, just two really big ones and one that looked awfully strange, like something big had hooked up with a Bassett or a Corgi, resulting in a relatively large head running around on a long torso with short feet.

Once Quinn got them to settle down, he pointed to them, starting with the largest. "That's Tiny, Rex, and Dublin. And to them, you probably smell like one giant steak, so they'll happily be your new best friends."

Putting out her hand, she gave them a chance to sniff her before giving them all a pet and a scratch, loving their happy energy and wagging tails. She hadn't pictured Quinn to be the type to have pets, and she loved that they were mutts. Probably shelter dogs. And damn if that didn't make her like Quinn all the more—a feeling she was still trying to fight. "They're really cute. I love dogs, but my hours are too crazy and my apartment's way too small."

"Well, you're welcome to hang out with these guys whenever you want. As for your apartment..." He pulled a set of keys off his keychain and offered them to her. "I want you to stay in my loft. It's in the building where I have my office so it'll be close to your restaurant, and I never use it for anything but to get changed before meetings, or if I'm having a really late night working."

She was already shaking her head, and he now had her wondering how smart it was to come here. "No way, Quinn. That's insane. You don't even know me. And what happens when you get tired of me and move on to dating supermodels again?"

"Then let me get to know you better—and you can still keep your apartment on the side if it'll give you some comfort to know it's there if you ever need it." He cupped her cheek, his green eyes so intense against his dark, roughed-up hair. "But you can't tell me your place is amazing when you don't even have hot water, and frankly, I don't like the fact that there isn't even a decent lock on the front door. It's not safe, Emma, and I'll be damned if I'm going to let anything happen to you. You either move into my apartment, or I'm buying your apartment building and renovating it."

"You *cannot* be serious. You realize that that's not normal, right? You've only just met me, Quinn. And you can't just buy the building I live in and renovate it because I don't have hot water and won't move into your loft. What the hell is wrong with you?" Not only should she not have come here, but it was a huge mistake. *Huge.*

"*What's wrong with me?*" He scoffed out a laugh and started to pace, looking like some madman, his height and build making the large space feel small as he towered over her, his muscular form coiled with tension. "What's wrong with me is that I can't get you out of my head, no matter how hard I try—and believe me when I tell you, *I've tried.* There's *no* way you should have this sort of effect on me, kitten, and yet I think about you constantly—and I worry about you. So, is it so wrong that I want to help you? I know this might seem like a lot to you, but from where I stand, it's nothing to buy your building or let you stay in my apartment."

"Or fix my fridge." She sighed, unsure of what to think especially after he'd confessed to so much.

"I like you, Emma. A lot. And just so we're clear, this *never* happens. *Not to me.* So don't go thinking you're just one of many. Because you're not. You're the only one."

8

QUINN WANTED TO GROAN. WHAT the hell was wrong with him? He knew she was far too independent to want to accept his help, but instead of taking things slow, he'd all but asked her to move in with him. Could he be any more stupid? Yet the woman made it so he couldn't think straight. All he wanted to do was ravage and possess her. Claim her as his own—just like she'd already laid a claim on him, making it so he didn't want anyone but her in his bed.

"Come on. Bath." He grabbed her hand and all but hauled her towards the master bedroom, all in an attempt to keep from ravaging her in his entry hall or doing anything more stupid than he'd already done.

She shrugged out of his grasp and stood her ground, looking at him with a scowl. "*Quinn...stop*. What the hell is wrong with you? You can't just push me around and make demands."

"New deal. I'll sign over not just your lease, but the real estate you currently rent for your restaurant. You'll own that part of the building free and clear so no one can ever take it away from you. But in exchange, I get you. Every part of you. However, whenever, and wherever I want you." He had to have lost his mind. There was no other logical explanation.

"You. Are. *Insane.*" And the way Emma was looking at him, Quinn had to wonder if she was right. "You need to take me home. *Right now.*"

"*No.* No fucking way." He ran a rough hand over his face and let out a weary sigh, his head and heart a jumbled mess. There was no way he could let her go when he so desperately wanted her, needed her. "After you take a bath. If you still want to go then, I'll take you home."

Without another word, and knowing full well that she might just walk out the door, he turned and walked towards the bath, hoping she'd eventually follow.

She didn't.

By the time he caught up to her, she was at the end of his driveway. "Emma...*stop.* For fuck's sake, don't make me toss you over my shoulder."

She kept going, completely ignoring him.

When he grabbed her hand and forced her to come to a standstill, she glared at him through her tears. "I can't do this, Quinn. I don't quite get what the hell it is you want from me, but I can't do it. You can't just buy me. That's not how I work—not even for my restaurant."

"I keep saying the wrong thing, Emma, and it's killing me to see you cry." He brushed her cheek dry, wondering how he could be such an idiot. "I don't know...maybe it's because I've spent the last decade dating women who only want something from me. But I really like you—*you and you alone.* I just don't know how to make things right between us."

It was hard for him to see her upset, and that, in and of itself, was damn curious, since he normally kept his distance, emotionally. He'd learned early on that caring about the women he dated only put him in a vulnerable position, and that was something he avoided at all cost. So then what the hell was it about Emma that was so different?

He frowned at her, suddenly annoyed with himself for wanting her so badly. And want her he did. More than anything—or anyone—he'd wanted in a very long time.

"Look…I appreciate your generosity, but when you tie it to sex or having me do what you want, it feels like you're just trying to buy me, instead of taking the time to get to know me and actually like me for who I am—as a person, and not just some passing fancy or obsession. And damn, Quinn—I *really* want to like you. But how the hell am I supposed to go there if I've been forced into it because of some agreement or struck bargain? It'll always get in the way."

He could be such an idiot where his emotions were concerned, which is why he preferred to treat his dealings with women as business transactions. With a deep sigh, he gently pulled her close and held her to him, relieved when she nestled against him instead of pulling away. "I want to let you set the pace, Emma, but I can't. I can't help myself where you're concerned, because you've gotten under my skin and I'll never have any peace until I've made you mine. My only excuse is that wanting you is screwing with my mind. But I won't take no for an answer—I can't. So if you don't want your restaurant tied to what we're doing here, then that's fine. I'll renew your lease. Give you whatever it is that you want. But I will have you, Emma. And I'll do whatever it takes to make sure you want me just as much as I want you."

Letting her off the hook for the restaurant was the only way—even if he lived to regret it. He couldn't let her walk out of his life, since every moment that passed, he found himself liking her more and more, even if *like* wasn't anywhere near a strong enough word. And though that might be insane—especially for him—he couldn't help himself. She'd been his only thought for months now, and he only wanted her more now that he'd gotten to know her better.

"Wow…that's some sort of declaration." She crossed her arms and gave him the sort of look one of her chefs would get when she was running her kitchen. And damn, but it was all he could do to not want to toss her over his shoulder and haul her to his bed. "So, then, how exactly does this play out if I say no to sleeping with you? I seriously don't think this whole alpha-male caveman crap includes rape, which means that you do *not* get to tell me how this is all going to go down. I tried that last night, and I wasn't really a fan since you decided to cut our night short."

"Fuck, Emma…" He ran his hands down his face, resisting the urge to scream. He'd hoped that by giving her just a tease of what he was capable of, she'd want him all the more. Instead, it'd backfired and she was holding it against him. "You're going to be the death of me. I don't know what it is you want me to do or say, but I'm a determined man, and I'll do whatever it takes."

Then, before she had a chance to respond or react, he pulled her to him, and kissed her as if they were the only two people on earth and their lives depended on it. His tongue found hers as she kissed him back with a passion he hadn't expected, yielding when he pushed and taking when he gave, her hands fisting his shirt, pulling him close. By the time he managed to break off their kiss, he knew he'd never stop craving her, like some drug that always left you wanting more than you could have, a drug you'd sacrifice your soul to have more of.

She was still clinging to him, her breathing heavy and her fingers knotted in the fabric of his shirt. Her heart was beating so fast…he could feel it pounding against his chest as he held onto her. "Why do you do this to me, Quinn?"

"I'm not asking for a lot, Emma…I just want to take care of you—and I want you in my bed. If you weren't being so goddamned stubborn about it, you'd probably find that you like being there." When she glared at him, he threw up his hands in frustration.

"It's not that I don't appreciate your help, Quinn. I do. Especially since you're offering to renew my lease without holding me to our prior agreement. But, shit…" She shook her head with a sigh. "You really know how to get my back up. And we still haven't taken the time to get to know each other."

"You know you're partly to blame for that, right?" He couldn't believe he was going to give in, but it seemed to be the only way. "What if you set the pace, then? I'm willing to give you that, as long as we eventually get to the point where you're in my bed. How's that?"

She shook her head, looking exasperated. "You're one hell of a stubborn man. You know that, right?"

"Not stubborn, darling. Desperate—and damned determined to have you, even if it takes me a little longer to get there." He ran his thumb across her cheek and stole another kiss, and then another, his forehead pressed to hers as he nuzzled her. "Come on, babe…I promised you a bath. Then once you're clean, we can swap stories and get to know each other better."

"Fine. But only because I'm too tired to keep arguing with you." Given that it was nearly one in the morning, he wasn't exactly surprised.

Holding her close and slowing his steps to match hers, his heart raced when she slipped her arm around his waist and let him lead her back to his home. And damn if he wasn't falling for her, lusting after her—and, at breakneck speed. There was a huge part of him that knew he'd get his heart trounced if he kept up this nonsense. And yet there was no stopping how he felt about her.

With the women he normally dated, he had no fear of getting emotionally vested or falling for them. No fear of doing or saying the wrong thing. And no fear of ever finding something meaningful. He knew Emma was worth the risk, because without her in his arms, in his life, there'd be no point in waking to face the day.

He closed the door behind them, but when she started to slip free of his grasp, he spun them around and pinned her to the door, making her breath catch in surprise. Nuzzling her, he nipped at her bottom lip and kissed her, his body aching from wanting her, like a piece of him was missing and would never feel whole until he'd had her.

His breathing was heavy when he finally managed to pull away. "I had to have just one last kiss before I let you set the pace." How he'd manage to actually let her do that, he hadn't a clue, especially when his need for her was running rampant. Not to mention, he liked to be in control—needed it. "I just don't know if I—"

Emma interrupted him, placing a gentle finger over his lips. "Quinn…I'm not some blushing virgin who doesn't want to be touched. And if the restaurant is no longer an issue, then I honestly have no desire to be the one setting the pace. If anything—especially after last night—I think I like it when you decide, as long as you're not holding back." She slipped out of his arms, still facing him, and pulled her t-shirt up over her head, a smile on her face, though his focus was on her perfectly full breasts, bound, not by some pretty lacy thing, but a sports bra. And damn if he didn't find that even sexier. "So what's it to be? Are you going to help me get clean, or do I need to take care of things myself?"

Hard as he was, he had to force himself not to ravage her right there on the hard entry floor with the dogs watching. And her words... She knew how he'd take them—and yet she'd gone there. He couldn't help but smile, his gaze taking her in. "And suddenly my woman is a tease..."

"Your woman, huh?" She flicked her eyebrows up teasingly, her large eyes filled with mischief and sparkling with humor. "I think I like that."

Scooping her into his arms, he tossed her over his shoulder, loving how she squirmed and laughed and screamed—especially when he bit her ass, now located all too conveniently. And when she smacked his ass in return, he knew they were in for a whole lot of fun.

It was hard to ignore her words as they repeated in his head. She wanted him to take control—wanted him to set the pace—now that she was no longer worried about her restaurant. And he could see why she might want someone else to take charge in the bedroom when she spent her entire work day in control and running every-thing—and everyone—around her. It would be his pleasure—and most definitely hers, by the time he'd had his way with her.

When he finally put her down in the spacious bathroom, he was taken by just how small she seemed, his height of six three towering over her petite frame. She held his gaze, her chest rising and falling, a delicious tension building between them as he took her in. Her tongue darted out and licked her bottom lip before she bit it for a moment—and damn but he felt his self-control slip.

Quickly, he got the hot water in the tub running, before turning back to more important matters like—ravaging Emma. He watched as she shimmied out of her jeans, her body perfectly proportioned with curves every woman should have.

With nimble fingers, he pulled her ponytail free and fisted his hand in her hair, dragging her up to him and covering her mouth in a bruising kiss as his tongue found hers. His cock strained against his jeans, growing up past the waistband, as her hips shifted against his length. One kiss led to another, his lips trailing down her neck as he nipped at her delicate skin, her back arching up as if in offering.

"Fuck, Emma...I want you." His words were spoken against her skin, between kisses. "But I'm not rushing this. By the time I finally take you, you're going to be begging me to fuck you, and by the time I'm through with you, I'll be sure you won't remember anyone who came before me. Are we clear?" She nodded, but it wasn't enough. He pulled her away, just enough to look her in the eyes. "Answer me."

She gave a little nod and bit her bottom lip again, making him want to kiss her. "Yeah, we're clear—though you're damn lucky I think it's hot when you get bossy."

He had to laugh. "I'm glad to hear it. Your bath's ready, though you're still wearing far too many clothes." Quinn rid her of her bra, releasing her gorgeous breasts, her nipples perfectly pink and already hard, begging to be sucked. Needing more, he let his fingers trail down between her breasts and over the swell of her belly, nuzzling her as he slipped her panties down over her hips and let them fall to the floor. "You're gorgeous, Emma. Stunning."

When she reached out to undo his jeans, he grabbed her wrist, eliciting a moan from her. "*Quinn...please.*"

He wanted to resist her, wanted to prolong the experience, their pleasure, but he'd never wanted anyone more than he wanted Emma in that moment. Letting her go, he sucked in a needy breath as she caressed him through his jeans before quickly setting him free. His erection thrust out into her hands, hard and engorged, pulsing with need and desire.

"Damn…you're big, Quinn." His cock jumped as she ran a gentle finger over the tip of his cock and down his length before going up onto the tips of her toes and kissing him, her lips warm and sweet as she slowly stroked him.

"Is that going to be a problem?" He sure as hell hoped not.

Her eyes sparkled with mischief as a smile tugged at her lips. "Definitely not where I'm concerned. Especially when it's all *mine*. Mine to fuck. Mine to taste…"

"*Fuck…*" Quinn groaned, letting their kisses linger a little longer before finding the strength to pull away and give her a stern look. "Into the bath with you, Ms. Sparrow."

"Only if you join me." She reached down and stroked him once more before stepping towards the bath, her eyes beckoning him to take her.

"At this point, I highly doubt I could deny you a single thing." He tossed his shirt aside, before ridding himself of his jeans, while watching her step into the large tub and slip under the water, emerging like a sea nymph, there to steal his heart.

With his cock aching for release, he joined her, the water steaming hot against his skin. The moment he sat down in one of the built-in seats, she pulled herself up to him and kissed him. And though he could feel her need, the passion in her kisses, he could also feel a hesitation there, an uncertainty that left him wondering. "Emma, I know I can be a pushy bastard, but you don't have to do this if you don't want to. Your restaurant is safe."

"Hush…" She kissed him again, slipping her leg across his hips and straddling him, his cock trapped between them as she rolled her hips and slid up and down his length. "I don't want to overthink what we're doing here, or I'm going to freak myself out and bolt. Though, crap…how does a condom work in water? It's safe on my end…I'm clean and on the Pill."

"Yeah… Completely safe here, too. You can trust me." He'd always used condoms. Always. But with Emma—he wanted her skin to skin. Wanted that trust between them. When she shifted her hips so the head of his cock caught at her entrance as she bit his lip, he could think of nothing but taking her. And yet... "Not yet... wait, sweetheart."

She groaned in protest but did as he asked, his cock throbbing against her opening. Raking his teeth against the slope of her neck, he slipped his hands down her sides and grabbed her hips tight in his grasp, his fingers digging into her soft flesh. "Tell me, Emma...tell me that you want me to fuck you."

Though he'd yet to take her, her breathing was heavy as she nuzzled him, trailing bites and kisses along his neck and jawline. "Please, Quinn...I need this. I need you."

"And do you trust me, darling?" He needed to know, though he was surprised it meant so much to him.

Her eyes locked on his, her breathing shallow. "Yeah...I do. Completely."

Thrusting up from under her, he pulled her down onto his cock, impaling her fully in one go as she cried out. She was mind-blowingly tight, and her body was forced to stretch around his girth. He could imagine the spark of pain mixing with her pleasure into one delicious sensation.

"Tell me again that you want me." He needed to make sure, because once he started to move, there'd be no hope of him stopping.

"I want you to fuck me, Quinn. I want you to fuck me until I don't even remember my name." Her hips tried to shift, but he held her still—though only for a moment more.

"You're so fucking naughty, kitten." With her still tight in his grasp, he started to rock her hips up and down his length. He caught her bottom lip between his teeth as she moaned into his mouth. Letting go of her, he trailed his hands up her back as her pace picked up, holding her down to him as he thrust up deep inside her. "Emma...you already have me so close. You and your perfectly sexy little body."

He sucked her nipple into his mouth and flicked it with his tongue, as she pressed her lips around her needy moans, her body tightening around him. Her breathing was now quick and shallow, her pace quickening as she curled her hips up and down his length, so her clit rubbed up against him. And then she was crying out as she came, her body quivering in his arms, tensing as her pleasure coursed through her.

Watching her come undone like that was more than he could handle and with just a few thrusts more, Quinn bit her shoulder and came, pulsing his cum deep inside her as she milked him, squeezing every drop from him, his head still spinning with his need for her.

Kissing her, he tried to catch his breath, and though he'd just come, he still needed her, wanted her, leaving him to wonder if he'd ever get his fill.

Somehow he doubted it.

9

LEANING BACK AGAINST QUINN'S CHEST, Emma closed her eyes as he shampooed her hair, his fingers working their magic to erase the day away. "You're spoiling me, Quinn. Between the scalp massage, the amazing sex, and best of all, the hot water, my real life's going to suck when I finally get back to it."

"If the hot water was the best part, then I need to try a hell of a lot harder." With his mouth at her ear, his words tickled her skin as he slipped his hand down between her legs to her still sensitive clit, and teased her until her head fell back against his shoulder and her breath caught.

It had been so incredibly long since she'd been with anyone, and it turned out that Quinn was an exceptional lover. Not that she'd expected anything less. From the moment she laid eyes on him, she knew he'd be mind-blowingly good in the sack—and damn, but he was exactly that.

"Maybe I'm just trying to goad you into fucking me again." When she spoke, her words came out on a needy breath, his fingers still stroking her clit, with slow, purposeful strokes, dipping inside her, teasing her towards yet another orgasm.

"Later. First I want to get to know a bit more about you. Remember?" He leaned over and kissed her cheek as he pulled his fingers free of her, leaving her unable to contain her moan in protest. "Isn't that what you wanted, kitten?"

"You really are a tease." She smiled at him over her shoulder and then pulled away enough to dip her head back into the water to rinse out the shampoo from her hair. Unable to stay away, she nestled back against his side, thinking herself damn lucky—and that wasn't something she'd expected. But Quinn wasn't just damn sexy and good-looking; it turned out that she'd been mistaken about him being a bastard.

Though she didn't think this would last more than a few dates— just long enough for him to grow bored with her—she told herself she'd be okay with that, since her life was too complicated for anything more. And yet she couldn't quite ignore the pang of disappointment that now resided in her chest.

"Tell me about yourself, love. Did you always want to be a chef?" He cupped her breast and rolled her nipple between his thumb and finger, so she felt a corresponding tug on her clit, making it pulse with an unfulfilled need, no matter that she'd already come.

She arched her back in response and took a deep breath, hoping she'd be able to answer him without moaning in the process. "I suppose so. My mom worked two jobs and my dad was long gone, so I was left to take care of my brother. He was a picky eater, so I got creative with the little we had and it turned out I was pretty good at coming up with combinations that worked well."

"We have that in common, you know. My dad died when I was ten and money was really tight. My mom worked several jobs to make ends meet, but we never did more than scrape by. Lived in a tiny two-bedroom apartment with my two brothers and my sister." He let out a weary sigh and kissed the top of her head. "Somehow we made it work."

No wonder he'd been so angry with her last night when she'd implied that he'd gotten everything he wanted by just taking it. She looked up at him with her brow furrowed. "I didn't realize, Quinn. And I was such a bitch to you yesterday. I'm sorry."

He brushed her cheek with a deep sigh. "Don't be. You didn't know—and I was being pushy."

"Well, you've come a long way." She was damned impressed that Quinn had gone from abject poverty to one of the wealthiest men on the East Coast. It said a lot about him.

He shifted her in his arms. "Come on. I'm not through with you yet, but I want you in my bed."

"I think I can live with that."

She was barely out of the tub and towel dry when Quinn pulled her to him, his lips hard on hers as his large, capable hands shifted her into his bedroom. His kisses were rough and demanding, and in that moment she was more than happy to give him anything he wanted. It was an unusual feeling for her to be willing to surrender so completely to what they were doing—to be willing to surrender to him, especially given their rocky and argumentative relationship. Yet his touch, his words, the way he made her feel, as if being with her was worth any sacrifice, made it so she could think of nothing but him.

"Do you trust me, Ms. Sparrow?" She loved all his little nicknames for her, but it was his words, spoken between kisses, that had her insides going liquid with the excitement and danger in his question.

They had spoken of trust earlier, but she knew he was asking her something different—and this was a different kind of trust. Her mind raced but could only come up with one answer. "Yeah, I do. Completely."

"Do you remember what you asked of me, sweetheart? To fuck you until you couldn't remember your name... Well, I'm about to do just that." He paused long enough to grab a silk tie from where it lay tossed aside on a chair.

"What's that for?" Excitement thrummed through her chest, along with a sliver of apprehension, the achy need between her legs growing, demanding release.

"I'm going to tie you up, my sweet girl." With one deft move-ment, he quickly had her wrists gently yet firmly bound, sending her heart hammering inside her chest. No one had ever tied her up before, but the mere thought of it had her thighs going slick. She was so wet, so ready to be on the receiving end of anything he had for her. "Do you have a problem with this?"

Her breathing was shallow as she looked into those green eyes of his, and shook her head. "I think I'd like it, though..." She suddenly felt shy—and damn if that wasn't something new too. "I really haven't done anything like this before, Quinn. I've only been with a few guys, but it was never anything too adventurous."

"But you do trust me?" When she took a deep breath and nodded, he nuzzled her, brushing his lips against hers, his stubble rough against her skin. "Then let me take care of you, Emma. And you can always tell me to stop. Always."

Quinn ran a finger down her lips before letting the tip slip in, as she sucked it into her mouth, eliciting a needy groan from him. With his eyes locked on hers and his gaze intense, he pulled free of her mouth and scooped her into his strong arms as if she weighed nothing. Positioning her on his bed, he raised her hands up over her head and tied her to his bed frame, her body squirming under him, already desperate to have him.

"Quinn...please." Propped up on his pillows, she rose up best she could to steal a kiss. It caught her somewhat off guard to find that she liked the feel of being restrained, and actually liked that she was at his mercy.

"Greedy little thing." He let his hand slowly trail up her thighs and between her legs so that by the time he ran his finger against her slick opening, her hips rose up to meet him in desperation. "Oh, Emma...you're so fucking wet. You love this, don't you?"

His two fingers slipped between her clit and pussy at a torturously slow pace, only dipping in enough to tease her towards insanity. Turning her head, she bit her arm to keep from moaning, as he nes-tled himself between her legs, his fingers still working her so that she ached almost painfully in her need for release.

Her arms pulled against her bindings as her body shifted, desperate for more, though being bound only served as a reminder that he was in control, increasing her need for him and making her want him all the more. "Please, Quinn...I can't take much more."

"Is this what you're looking for?" He buried his fingers deep inside her as his mouth clamped on her swollen clit, and she swore she nearly came from a single flick of his tongue. His fingers thrust in and out of her with slow purpose as he nipped and sucked at her clit, and his free hand reached up to tease her nipple, his stubble adding yet another sensation as it gently scraped against her delicate skin. And when he pressed a finger against the bud of her ass, her orgasm tore through her like a runaway freight train. Just like that.

Yet he was far from done with her, and though she'd just come, she was already desperate for more of him, happy to take everything he had to give, her head dizzy with her need and the late hour.

Shifting up from between her legs, he straddled her waist, and with a hand on the headboard, he leaned forward to run his rock-hard cock along her lips as her tongue darted out to lick him. At the first touch of her tongue, his cock jumped, his eyes half closed, his look utterly sensual. And when he spoke, his voice was so thick with need, it only spurred her on further, increasing her need for him. "Tell me, sweetheart...do you want a taste?"

Propped up as she was on the pillows, she not only had a perfect view of his washboard abs, but was also positioned perfectly to take him. She didn't bother to answer his question but rather leaned forward and wrapped her lips around his thick cock, flicking her tongue over its silky surface, tasting his masculine essence.

"Fuck, Emma, that's so damn good." His hips shifted towards her, forcing her to take more of him as he brushed the hair from her face, his gaze watching every detail of her expression.

Pinned as she was against the pillow, she was at his mercy as he thrust forward, working his cock as he fucked her mouth and she sucked him, wanting everything he had to give her. She watched the tension in his face, in his body, as if he was trying to hold himself back, even as she tried to quicken his pace, desperate for more of him.

He groaned and pulled free of her, leaving her to whimper in protest. "Quinn…"

"It was too fucking good, love. And I'm not through with you yet." Her bindings were just loose enough to allow him to flip her onto her hands and knees, and slick as she was, he buried himself in one go, a needy cry escaping Emma's lips as her body stretched tight around his thick girth and long length, filling her completely—and then some.

With each thrust, he ground his hips against her, and though he couldn't possibly get any closer, she still wanted even more of him. He leaned forward, his chest pressed to her back as he wrapped an arm across her breasts. He clamped his hand around her neck as he arched her head backward, stealing a greedy kiss. His tongue thrust into her mouth, echoing the way his cock fucked her pussy, leaving her body to tighten deliciously around him. The intensity of his every action had her teetering on the edge again, and when his pace quickened, she couldn't help but cry out, her body tensing in his arms as she came again, his own release following hers with just another thrust.

"Emma…" His breathing was heavy as he shifted his weight off her and held her close, her arms still bound. "I swear, love…I don't think I'll ever get my fill."

⚜

Emma awoke in Quinn's arms, her head heavy from their late night together, and her body deliciously sore from him taking her again and again into the early hours of the morning. Without a doubt, she'd never had more amazing sex—or as much of it—and yet, there was a flutter of panic in her chest. *What the hell was she doing?*

She really liked Quinn, and she'd figured a bit of great sex would go a long way, given her lack of a love life. But already, this was far more intense than anything she'd planned on, and it wasn't as though she didn't know Quinn's reputation. What did she think would come from this? Nothing but a broken heart at the rate she was falling for him. She had to put some distance between them before she ended up getting in way too deep.

She had to go. There was no other choice.

He was still sound asleep when she slipped out of his arms and got dressed, needing to escape before he awoke. It was a crap thing to do, but she knew if she stuck around, he'd manage to talk her into staying, like some snake charmer putting her under his spell.

Quinn stirred and turned towards her. "Hey...come back to bed, kitten. It's lonely without you in my arms."

Damn, but he looked sexy with his hair all tousled and his stubble now thick. "I'm sorry but I really have to go. I've got to get to work so I'm just going to call a cab. Go back to bed, Quinn."

"I can drive you back." He started to get out of bed when she took a step back.

"No. I can manage just fine on my own, okay?" She wanted to groan at the sound of panic in her voice.

"Then at least take my SUV. I've still got my bike and the Aston for getting around. I'll just swing by the restaurant to get the keys later." He padded over to where he'd tossed his jeans, and dug out his keys.

Emma's gaze felt glued to his fit body and hardening cock, but before she did something she'd regret, she snagged his keys, gave him a quick peck on the cheek, and bolted for the door, ignoring him as he called out to her.

10

"YOU LOOK LIKE SHIT, MAN." Gabe gave his brother a smug grin as he sat across from Quinn's desk. "Must have been one hell of a fun night."

Quinn glared at him, still in a mood after Emma all but bolted out of his home earlier that morning. "I don't want to talk about it. Just make sure you get your hands on that property I emailed you about the other night. I want it done ASAP, and it'll need a major overhaul. Spare no expense, and if you have any questions, find me."

"Yeah. Here's a question for you." Gabe flipped through some papers. "Why the hell did you have me buy a residential rental property on the outskirts of town? I bought it for cash yesterday, and picked up the permits this morning. We can get started on Monday, though you know as well as I do that it's a crap investment."

"I've got my reasons." Quinn checked the time. He still had a whole day ahead of him before he'd get the chance to see Emma. Maybe if he swung by the restaurant before dinner, he could catch her before things got crazy for her with the evening rush. Not that there was any hope of him getting anything done, his mind

too distracted to focus. Memories of his night with her kept playing in his head on an endless loop, leaving him desperate to have
her again.

He'd been with his fair share of women, but damn, being with
Emma had been an experience unlike any he'd had before. Emma
had been an equal participant, utterly responsive and willing to give
and take pleasure, unabashedly. Usually it felt like most of his dates
were there just to get themselves off and take care of his needs as
payback for a generous evening out. Except that his needs were only
ever superficially met. With Emma? He couldn't remember the last
time he'd felt so alive, so complete.

And that was a huge problem if she was trying to avoid him.

"*Oi!* Earth to Quinn." Gabe shook his head when Quinn finally
focused on him. "What's gotten into you? You're never distracted—
especially not at work."

Though Quinn was the prime driving force behind his company,
having made several wise investments which gave him the money
needed to fund further projects, Gabe was his right hand when it
came to running and building their business, while his other brother,
Morgan, researched new business ventures and investment opportunities. Together, they were a great team, each of them focused and
driven—except when Quinn was pining over a woman who couldn't
get out of his bed fast enough.

He just didn't get it.

Most women loved it when he took an interest in them, and he'd
never had anyone complain about him trying to help out financially.
So why the hell did it infuriate Emma? He knew what it was like to
not have the funds when the bills kept coming, and he was happy
to take some of that off her plate. Yet it did nothing but piss her off.

"I don't know...I guess my mind's just elsewhere today." He
checked the time and wondered what Emma was doing. *Damn it.*

"Don't suppose it has anything to do with this building you had
me buy?" When Quinn glared at him, Gabe laughed and shook his
head. "Who are you trying to help, Quinn?"

"You think you're just so fucking smart, huh?" Quinn tried not to give anything away, but he knew Gabe wasn't buying it.

"It's like those strays of yours. But you can't save every mutt out there—just like you can't keep everyone's troubles from creeping up on them by buying and renovating their buildings." Gabe ran a rough hand across his stubbly jaw. "At least we're on track for the Rush Street project. Everything's been finalized and our investors are excited to have it completed."

"Wait…Rush Street?" *Fuck!* That was the building with Emma's restaurant. "What the hell do you mean it's been finalized? We have another month before we sign off on that deal. I've made other plans for one of the storefronts."

"*Quinn.* You're fucking killing me. Everything's been finalized, man. One of the investors had to bump up the date so he could take off to China, and since there wasn't any reason to delay it and everyone else was fine with signing early, I took care of it. There's no way to change the plans now. It's not going to happen—and our investors aren't people we want to jerk around or piss off." Gabe shook his head and cursed under his breath.

Fuck. Quinn hadn't expected Gabe to push the plans through so quickly. He couldn't do this to Emma. Not when he'd given her his word. "Do what you have to do to make it happen, Gabe. I *need* that storefront. It's important, okay?"

"I'll see if there's anything I can do to persuade them to change their minds, but this is business and it's a done deal, so I make no promises. You've been distracted, Quinn—and it's affecting your game. And maybe soon, your reputation." Gabe got to his feet, shaking his head and tapping the papers Quinn gave him on the edge of the desk. "You know where to find me if you need to talk."

Quinn tried to clear his head and wrap up the contracts he'd been trying to work on, though all he'd managed to do was wrestle with his thoughts of Emma. There was no way he could go back on his promise to her. That just wasn't an option. Not when he was finally getting somewhere with her. Yet, he knew that these sorts of deals could be complicated and it was pretty much a certainty that he was fucked. All he could do was try to make it happen, and if not, he had to find an alternative.

Finally giving up, he turned to his computer and pulled up her lease, making the necessary changes that would extend Emma's lease on the restaurant. He'd given her his word, and he couldn't have her second-guessing him. He knew he was taking a huge risk with the latest developments, but he would find a way to make it work. He *had* to. And yet…knowing there was a chance he might have to break his word to her, it'd be irresponsible for him to not put a clause in. If need be, he'd move her restaurant. A better location, no expense spared. And in the meantime, he'd do his damnedest to make sure she could keep her space.

By the time the day wrapped up, Quinn couldn't wait any longer to see Emma. He was completely distracted and tense, desperate to see her after the way she'd left. He needed to know where things stood—and needed to make sure he did whatever it took to get her back in his bed. One night had been nowhere near enough.

When he arrived at the restaurant, there were a handful of diners there catching an early meal, and the hostess, having recognized him, was happy to point him towards the kitchen. Excitement thrummed in his chest as he looked for Emma in the open kitchen—only to find her sitting at a table with a good-looking man, her head propped against his shoulder as she laughed and kissed his cheek, her hands wrapped around his muscular arm.

It struck him that he'd never seen her look so carefree and genuinely happy, and damn, but that only added to the sudden jealousy that reared deep inside his chest. The thought of her with another man, with another man touching her, tasting her, fucking her… It didn't matter that they'd only been on a few dates: in his head, to his body, in his *heart*, she was already his—and his alone. Every cell in his body wanted to claim her as his own, wanted to possess her so she could think of no other man but him.

Yet he had to wonder…was this other man the reason she'd left in such a hurry? Had she lied about not being in a relationship?

He'd fucking murder the bastard for touching her, for taking her away from him.

He thought about walking out of there without saying a word, but he wanted to see how she'd react. All he'd asked for was honesty between them, and he wanted her to know she'd been caught.

Doing his best not to deck the guy, he approached the table, her paperwork in hand. "I don't mean to interrupt your date, but I thought you might want a copy of your new lease."

He tossed the papers onto the table in front of her, despite wanting to keep a cool head, and then spun around to leave as she called out to him. It didn't take long for her to catch up to him and grab his arm, but he was damned if he could control his jealousy. "Now's not a good time, Emma. Just go back to your boyfriend there."

"Ew!" She was already dragging him off to a quiet area where they could be alone. "That boyfriend just so happens to be my brother, Nate—and you'd know that if you'd stuck around long enough for me to introduce you, instead of taking off like a jealous ass."

Her brother.

He wanted to groan. She couldn't have been more right—he had been a jealous ass. "Well, I wouldn't be acting like a jerk if you hadn't bolted out of my bed this morning. What the hell was that about?"

Her eyes clouded over as she looked away and said nothing for far too long. "What does it matter, Quinn? It's not like I have any delusions about your lifestyle. I know that I'm one of many and what we have is short-lived."

It wasn't as though he could deny his past relationships, and yet things felt completely different with Emma. "That's my past, Emma, and I've done nothing to make you think that there's anyone else or that I'm looking for a quick fling. Am I not allowed to want more?"

"Your past—as in…what? A week ago?" She shook her head and backed away. "Look, I get that you want more, but my life is too crazy for me to be taking those sorts of risks. And you *are* a risk, Quinn, because after last night…" She let out a weary sigh and looked away from him. "I could really fall for you."

"For fuck's sake, Emma, then take a chance. What do you have to lose?" The woman was making him crazy.

"My heart and my independence, for starters." She shook her head and turned away from him, but he was having none of it.

"I refuse to let you go without trying to make this work." He couldn't quite believe he was going down this road, but he couldn't get her out of his head. Cupping her face in both his hands, he pulled her close and kissed her, sweet and tender, his lips lingering on hers as if she was the only thing that could sustain him. "I don't care if it sounds insane—and I don't blame you for doubting this could work—but I don't give up easily, and I'm not taking no for an answer. Not until you've given us a fair shot."

"If Emma says no, then that's the answer you're taking, whether you like it or not." Anger laced the newcomer's voice, and Quinn turned to find, not just her brother, but Emma's sous chef, Jake.

Perfect. What a way to win her over and make a good impression on her friends and family. Well, he didn't care. Emma was all that mattered.

However, he hadn't expected Emma to step up to them. "I appreciate you worrying about me, but this doesn't concern either one of you. I can take care of myself."

"No one's saying you can't, Em." Jake shook his head at Emma and then shot Quinn a glare. "But we're not—"

"But you're not going to get involved in something that's none of your business. Now if the two of you don't mind, I'm trying to have a private conversation." Emma was certainly in her no-nonsense chef mode, and he doubted there were many who'd stand up to her when she was like this.

And damn, but that was a total turn-on. He'd always been authoritative and in control, whether with business or women, but he liked that Emma was just as headstrong as he was, and the challenge she offered him. Yet, annoying her brother and friend wouldn't do him any good either.

He ran a gentle hand down her arm. "They're just worried about you, Emma. And rightfully so, since they don't know me. I had just wanted to drop off your new lease—not to interrupt your time with your brother. I'll swing by later when you get off work."

She pursed her lips as if thinking it over and then nodded. "I still have your car, so I'll drop by your house with it."

Not exactly an enthusiastic yes, but he'd take anything he could get right about now. "Look over the lease and let me know if you have any questions. I'll see you later, love." He kissed her, letting his lips linger, marking her as his since he knew full well that Jake was watching. "Gentlemen." With a brief nod in their direction, he headed out the door.

Except that a simple getaway wasn't in the cards for him that evening. He walked out into the brisk evening air and ran into the one person he truly despised, ruining his budding good mood as he cursed under his breath.

"Ryker…" Vince Capaldi shook his head with a cocky smile. "Back at the Old Port again? You're starting to become a creature of habit. Is my restaurant not good enough?"

"I like the steak here. You should try it." Quinn tried to rein in his annoyance, not wanting Capaldi to see he'd had any effect on him.

Though Capaldi had a few restaurants in Portmore—one just down the street, as a matter of fact—he also made a variety of other investments, which often led to him and Quinn bidding on similar properties and contracts. Yet it was his supposed ties to the mob and the fact that Capaldi was a complete ass that fueled his dislike of the man.

"Probably doesn't hurt that the chef's a looker." Capaldi gave him a shit-eating grin, while tilting his head towards Emma, who could still be seen through the large glass windows of the restaurant. "That piece of ass? I'd have her bent over on all fours as I gave it to her good. And it'd serve her right for opening up this yuppie dump next to my place."

Quinn saw red as the image of Capaldi fucking Emma invaded his mind. "You fucking bastard…"

"Hit a nerve, did I? So, you're fucking that ballsy whore? Well, by the time I'm through giving it to her—"

Quinn's fist connected with Capaldi's fat face, his muscles coiled and ready to attack again, as the man reeled backward. "You touch her, you so much as look in her direction, and I'll fucking kill you."

Capaldi wiped the blood from his split lip. "You'll pay for this, Ryker. I'll burn you and everything you own and care about to the fucking ground."

"I'd like to see you try." Quinn dodged Capaldi's blow and pushed him aside, just as Emma and Jake burst out of the restaurant.

Jake made a grab for Capaldi, as Quinn stood in front of Emma to keep her from getting hurt. Capaldi wasn't exactly fit, but he was a big man, and though Jake seemed capable of leveling him, Quinn wasn't taking any chances. "Get inside, Emma."

"What the hell is going on here?" Emma was tugging at his arm, trying to get answers.

"This isn't fucking over, Ryker. You and your whore will both pay." Capaldi shrugged free of Jake's grasp and stalked his way across the road, his curses shattering the quiet of the evening.

With Capaldi gone, Quinn turned around to face Emma, his heart racing as Capaldi's threat ran through his head. He cupped her cheek and stole a quick kiss. "I swear, if that bastard comes near you, I'll fucking kill him."

"What the hell happened? Are you okay?" Emma searched his face, looking worried for him. And damn, but it made him happy that she cared.

"I'm fine, love. I'll let you get back to work, but if Capaldi shows up again, you're to call me immediately." He'd murder the bastard if he laid a finger on her.

"I don't know what happened between you and Capaldi, but he's not an enemy you want." She shook her head, her eyes filled with worry for him.

"I'd take on an army of men like Capaldi to keep you safe, Emma. He's been warned."

11

"I DON'T WANT TO HEAR IT—FROM either of you. My personal life is no one's business but my own." With the adrenaline still racing through Emma's body from the fight, she was in no mood to be grilled by her brother and Jake, her emotions running high.

"We're just worried about you, Em." Nate grabbed her hand and gave it a squeeze. "I don't know him, but the fact that he's brawling on the sidewalk outside your restaurant doesn't exactly impress me."

"I don't know what they were fighting about, but I can tell you that the guy Quinn punched is the biggest ass I know. And you know what? Quinn's been nothing but helpful and considerate and sweet." How the hell was it that she was now defending Quinn, when just days ago, she'd thought him a bastard?

"Well, you know him best, Em. And I know better than to tell you what to do." Nate grabbed his jacket and shrugged into it, his movements still stiff and painful from the accident.

She had to resist the urge to reach out and help him, knowing it'd only frustrate him that he needed help for such a simple act. That was why it was so important that he get the type of physical therapy he so desperately needed—and soon. The longer they let things go, the more permanent the damage could become. Not to mention, he was a shadow of his former self, the carefree man she loved now haunted by far too much. And it was killing her to see him like that.

"Call and let me know what the doctor says. And if you need me to come with you, I can get someone to cover me here."

"I will, but you worry too much, and I can make it on my own." He kissed her cheek, and then turned to Jake. "Thanks for keeping an eye on her."

"For all the good it does." Once Nate was on his way, his limp a bit better than it'd been, Jake turned back to her. "So, Ryker renewed the lease?"

"Yeah. I guess he did." Just like he'd promised. She let out a sigh, a weight lifting off her chest, though that fight with Capaldi was still nagging at her.

Jake hung his head with a shake before looking up at her through those thick lashes of his. "Do I want to know what you did to secure the lease?"

"I know what you're implying—and the answer is no, I didn't sleep with him to get the lease. He'd already agreed to renew it beforehand. Not that it's any of your business."

"So you *did* sleep with him… Fucking great." Hands on his hips, Jake started to pace a tight circle, looking ready to punch something.

"Look, my love life's already pathetic enough without getting rid of the only guy who's shown me any interest." She was so frustrated, she could scream.

"You know he's not the only one who's interested." Jake reached out and cupped the back of her neck, his intense gaze lingering on her eyes, her lips.

"You're my best friend, Jake." She let out a weary sigh, reaching up to hold his forearm, locking the two of them together. Anything else beyond their friendship would be far too awkward and uncomfortable. "We should get back to work. Things are starting to pick up."

The night ended up being a blur, which wasn't terribly unusual for a Saturday night. At least it kept her mind off Quinn—and Capaldi—though Jake was still in a mood when service ended.

She pulled off her chef's whites and tossed them in the laundry, her mind immediately straying to Quinn, that glorious tub of his, and all that steamy, hot water. Her body had been deliciously sore all day long, acting as a constant reminder of their time together. She'd thought that sleeping with him would scratch that itch and give her some relief. Instead, she found herself constantly running through her memories of their night together and desperately wanting more.

Maybe she'd head home first to shower, so she'd be less tempted to take him up on whatever it was he was offering. Her shower would be pathetic, cold and dull in comparison to Quinn's bath, but at least she wouldn't be growing more attached to a man who could trounce her heart. All she had to do is just drop off the car and get the hell out of there.

"It's been a long night." Emma leaned against the counter, wanting to smooth things over between herself and Jake before she left for the night, though she wasn't quite sure how to go about it. "Jake... you know our friendship means the world to me."

"Yeah, I know." He let out a sigh, and pulled her into a one-armed hug. "I'm sorry if I'm a pain in the ass, but I don't want to see you get hurt, Em. And Quinn Ryker? Of all the guys to hook up with... you know his reputation."

"I just can't overthink this right now, okay?" She shifted out of his arms, trying to stay positive. "At least the restaurant's safe. We'll still have a job and a paycheck, and I can get my brother the help he needs. That's got to count for something."

"I could help with money, you know. Anything you need, Em." He unbuttoned and pulled off his whites, bundling the fabric into a ball, showing off his muscular arms and broad shoulders.

"I know—and I appreciate it." Yet she couldn't go there. Money had a way of ruining things, and she refused to risk their friendship.

"You're dropping off his car, right? Do you want me to follow you to his house so you have a ride back?"

"Thanks for the offer, but it's late and I want to swing by my place first. You should head home—make the most of your days off." With Sundays and Mondays having the slowest trade, she'd opted to close the restaurant on those days. It was an arrangement that seemed to work well enough, giving everyone the chance to recover without having to keep too many employees rotating through the schedule, and on the payroll.

"Em…" He let out a deep breath, though there was resignation in his lax stance. "Call me if you need anything."

Sweaty and stinking of food, Emma was desperate for a shower— even if it was a quick one—and clean, comfy clothes. She wouldn't take long, and then she could drop by Quinn's. At least that way, she wouldn't be tempted to hop into his bath and bed, since there was a far better chance of her thinking clearly if she wasn't naked with his amazing cock pressing against her with the promise of all it was capable of. She quickly locked up and set off home.

Parking outside her building, she got ready to let herself in when she spotted a formal-looking piece of paper taped to the inside window of the entry. A building permit—with Ryker Investments listed as the owner of the property.

Bastard.

Well, Quinn sure as hell moved quickly. She'd give him that. He no doubt pulled more than a few strings to get the sale and permits put through—even though she told him not to do this very thing. There was a small part of her that thought it chivalrous and romantic that he'd put such an effort and expense into making sure she was taken care of, but the part of her that was pissed off at him was far bigger at the moment. Why the hell couldn't he just leave it alone?

She quickly showered—in lukewarm water, curse him—and then threw on jeans and a sweater, knowing there was a chill in the night air. As late as it was, there weren't many other cars on the dark, winding road that ran by the ocean and Quinn's home. Though his car was damn nice and luxurious, it wasn't a vehicle she was used to and she'd be happy to hand over the keys and get back to her old Honda. Luckily, she found herself pulling down Quinn's drive no more than fifteen minutes later.

Quinn answered his door with his dogs waiting patiently behind him, their tails wagging with restrained anticipation. "Sweetheart..." He leaned in, cupped her cheek and gave her a lingering kiss filled with passion, before stepping aside to let her in. Something—the glare, her rigid stance, her scowl—must have tipped him off to her bad mood. "Is everything okay?"

She handed him a zipped plastic bag filled with beef bones for the dogs, though she did her best to hold onto her anger. "Can you please explain to me why there's a building permit taped to the window of my apartment building with your company's name on it?"

"Damn, that was fast." He ran a hand across his chin. "Thanks for the bones, by the way. You may just be the mutts favorite person right about now."

"Still waiting, Quinn..." She wanted answers and refused to let him distract her.

His jaw tightened and he took a step forward, his gaze locking on hers. "Your apartment has no security to speak of, you don't even have basic necessities, and that landlord of yours had no interest in making the repairs your place needed. So don't you dare get angry with me, Emma. You know I want you safe. I had no choice but to buy the place, though why you'd stay there to begin with, I haven't a clue."

"I stay there because the rent's cheap and I don't have billions warming my bank account." She groaned, knowing she sounded like a jerk. As if it was his fault that she had money problems. "I'm sorry that I'm being a bitch, but all my savings went into opening the restaurant, and then..." She shook her head, not wanting to get into her brother's issues, though she was helpless to keep her eyes from stinging with the emotion of it all.

"Emma..." His attitude softened. He pulled her into his arms and held her there, enveloping her in his muscular embrace. She should have been pushing him away, but at that moment, she'd happily stay nestled against his arms for an eternity, the steady rhythm of his heart soothing her. "Come on, love."

Still holding onto her, Quinn steered them towards the great room and sat them down on the soft leather sofa, tucking her in against his side.

Emma sighed and rested her head on his shoulder. "It's not that I don't appreciate your help, but my problems aren't your concern."

"That's not how I work. You can fight me all you want on it, but it's not going to change a thing. What sort of a jerk would I be if I let you live in a place that doesn't even have decent hot water? And like you said, I have plenty of money sitting in my bank account, so I might as well put it to good use—even if it pisses you off." He tipped her head back and kissed her, looking all too cocky.

She glared at him, though there wasn't a whole lot of anger behind it. "You're too used to getting your way. You know that, right?"

"Good. Because I have every intention of continuing that trend with you in my bed." He rose to his feet and scooped her into his muscular arms, making her curse.

She pounded on his chest, though she might as well be pounding on a rock. "Put me down, Quinn. I'm still mad at you."

"Mmm…I like angry sex. All that heat and passion." He nipped at her bottom lip, the flicker of delicious pain going straight to her aching clit. "Do you like it a bit rough, sweetheart? Do you like a bit of pain with your pleasure?"

"Fuck, Quinn." She could already feel herself getting wet. She had no doubt that this would be a battle she'd be losing.

"I want an answer, Ms. Sparrow—and I don't like to be left waiting." He tossed her onto his bed and stripped off his t-shirt, making it impossible for her to ignore his washboard abs—abs she would happily lick like a Popsicle dripping on a hot summer day.

Reaching down, he slipped his fingers into her hair and fisted it, pulling her towards him for a hungry kiss, their tongues clashing as her hands undid his jeans as if of their own volition, ignoring all logical thought.

He roughly pulled her away, a hunger in his eyes that had her insides going liquid. "Answer me, Emma."

When she tried to close the distance between them, he tightened his hold, making it clear that she'd get nowhere until she'd given him what he wanted. She thought about his question, and realized that she didn't have enough experience to know exactly what she did or didn't like, even if she had her suspicions.

"I've never done this sort of thing before, but…yeah, I think I'd like it." It was hard to get the words out and admit such a thing, but she was quickly realizing that Quinn was awakening a part of her that she'd never realized had existed until now. He'd turned her into a creature far more sexual than she could have ever imagined herself to be.

"Good. Because I want you so bad, I don't think I can take this slow or be gentle. Not right now. Not when I need you down to the marrow of my bones." He kissed her then, hard, his tongue warring with hers as he groaned into her mouth, breaking their kiss only long enough to yank her sweater up over her head.

Her hands fumbled with his jeans, desperate to free his thick cock as it pressed against her in promise, a teaser of all the pleasure that was to come, her body aching with a newfound yearning for him. Pushing her back, he yanked off the rest of her clothing and then his, tossing it aside, before lifting her further up unto the bed and covering her body with his.

He bit her neck, sending a sharp jolt of need down her spine and to her aching clit as she cried out in a needy whimper and wrapped her legs around his hips to pull him close. Yet he didn't enter her, but locked his eyes with hers, his gaze intense. "Say it, Emma. Tell me that you want me. Because, fuck…I've never wanted anyone more. You're all that matters, love."

His admission, his vulnerability, tore at her defenses so she couldn't help but let him into her heart, even if she wasn't ready to admit to anything but the physical. "I want you, Quinn. I need you, ache for you. Desperately."

He buried himself with one deep thrust, his teeth sinking into her neck, so the flicker of pain mingled with her pleasure into an overwhelming need for more. Her hips rose up to meet him as he took her roughly, grabbing her ass to bury himself deeper, his fingers digging into her flesh. Each thrust hammered into her, and yet it still wasn't enough. With his head bent to hers, he covered her mouth in a kiss that stole her breath and swallowed her moans, as the energy built inside her, coiling in on itself and readying to explode in its release.

She was so close…and then he was pulling out of her, flipping her onto her front, and pulling her ass up to him as he plunged in deep from behind, filling her so completely. "You're so fucking wet, sweetheart."

His words had her going even wetter still, and when he fisted her hair in one hand, pulling her head back while driving into her with his other hand clamped around her breasts, she nearly came. She couldn't wrap her head around the effect he had on her, but it was as if he knew her better than she knew herself. And it seemed that whatever he had to give, she was happy to be on the receiving end of it.

He leaned forward, his mouth at her ear so that his warm breath sent a shiver down her spine as he continued to drive into her, one forceful thrust after the other. "Tell me you're mine, Emma."

"Fuck, yes…I don't want anyone else, Quinn." And then she was coming, and he was coming with her, her orgasm crashing through her, even as she wondered about the words she'd just spoken.

12

WITH HIS ARM AROUND HER waist, Quinn pulled Emma close, her still naked body fitting perfectly against him as he spooned her from behind. He was trying to give her the chance to recover from their lovemaking, trying to suppress his insatiable need for her, trying to resist the urges of his mind and body to fuck her once more.

Leaning forward, he kissed her shoulder and neck, his desire for her already stirring again, despite his best intentions. "Emma, I know we haven't been together long, but you're the only one I want to be with. And after thinking you were on a date with another man...I want it to be just the two of us. No one else."

She turned in his arms to face him, her hazel eyes darkening. "I have no interest in seeing anyone else. But with that said, my life's too crazy for any sort of relationship. I'm swamped with everything I have to do at the restaurant. It's not just cooking, but inventory, accounting...there isn't time for anything else."

Hell, that was an easy enough problem to solve. "I can help you with that, kitten. My accountant is a whiz, and I'll find you someone top-notch to take care of inventory. I could even speak with Finn if you'd like. Have him take over some of your shifts—or get you a different chef to help you out."

"Quinn..." She shook her head and laughed. "That's really sweet of you, but I don't think you get it."

"How can you say that when I started with nothing? I know what it's like to work your ass off, to try to build your business from the ground up. But if I can help—which I can—then why not let me? It doesn't lessen your accomplishments—and it'll give me what I want, which is more time with you." He had to wonder if that was part of it. As if her success wouldn't count unless she was constantly busting her ass.

"I can't afford that sort of help—and before you offer, I can't have you paying for it either. I don't want your money." She cupped his cheek and brushed his lips with a lingering kiss that stirred his need for her. "You're a good man, though. A far cry from the bastard I'd first thought you to be."

His eyes narrowed as he gave it all some thought—not the part where she'd thought him a bastard, which he could certainly be at times, but rather her lack of income. "Feel free to tell me it's none of my business, but your restaurant's successful, and you don't exactly live an extravagant lifestyle, so I'd think you'd have it in your budget to get the help you need. Not that I wouldn't pay for it in a heartbeat, if you'd let me."

He hadn't expected her eyes to tear up. "There are other circumstances that have made money difficult."

It was killing him to see her hurting like this, and the fact that she wouldn't let him help her was infuriating. "Emma...talk to me, love. For fuck's sake, don't shut me out."

She looked away and squeezed her eyes shut, and for a moment, he thought she was going to grab her clothes and leave. Instead, she turned back to him and nestled against his shoulder. "It's my brother. A drunk driver hit him and he nearly didn't survive it. He's had multiple surgeries and he's in physical therapy, but the insurance company won't pay for anything but the most basic care, and the guy who hit him was uninsured and out of state, so it's been impossible to try to collect any money from that end. Whatever money I do make, I give to Nate for physical therapy, since he doesn't make enough on his own to cover it all. The cost is exorbitant."

No wonder she'd been so desperate to hold onto the lease—and why she'd been so hesitant to get on his bike. It all made sense now. And yet this was just one more thing he could help her with, if only she'd let him. He had to find a way to ease the weight of all she was carrying on her shoulders, whether she agreed to it or not.

"I'm sorry about your brother, but I can help you both. It'll be okay, love." He tightened his hold on her until she was nestled securely in his arms. "Though I think it's time we struck another deal."

"*Quinn...*" She all but groaned as she tried to pull away from him. Not that he was letting her go anywhere. "Your deals do nothing but infuriate me."

"Well, if you weren't so stubborn and would let me help you every now and then, then I wouldn't be forced into bartering or blackmailing you into seeing reason." The fire in her eyes left him wanting to fuck her yet again, even though he knew he'd only want her more, when all was said and done.

She may have turned him down before, but he knew she wouldn't be able to walk away from the offer he was about to make her. "I'd like to pay for all your brother's medical bills. I'll find him the best doctors out there, and if there's anything at all that can be done to help improve his condition, I'll do it."

He heard her breath catch as she looked up at him, her eyes shimmering as her tears threatened to spill over. "You'd do that for me—for Nate?"

Gently, he brushed her cheek and kissed her. "I would. You have my word."

"So, what's the catch? What's it in exchange for?" He saw her hesitation, but he had to push that aside since he knew they were perfect for each other—more so since he'd gotten to know her better. He just had to help her see it.

"You'll move in with me—and you'll let me help you with the running of the restaurant by funding you as a silent partner." He put his hand up to stifle her protests. "I already own the building, and this way, you'll have use of the space rent-free, and I'll also be able to give you the help you need to manage the place without running yourself ragged in the process."

"I want nothing more than to help my brother, but how the hell can I agree to that? Your offer's beyond generous, but having you as a partner in the restaurant…" She took a deep breath, letting it out in ragged bursts. "It won't work. Not when your interest in the restaurant is tied to a relationship that you'll eventually tire of."

"That's unfair, Emma. I'm not going to deny being with more than my share of women, but my feelings for you are completely different than the way I've felt for anyone else." Didn't she realize what she meant to him? And yet he'd never fully admitted his feelings for her, even to himself. "I'm falling for you, Emma. I know we haven't known each other long—"

"*At all*, Quinn. We don't know each other at all." She cupped his cheek, and he couldn't help but lean into her touch and kiss her palm, eliciting a sigh. "And you *can't* be falling for me. This isn't some fairy tale."

"Time doesn't matter when it comes to love—and I meant what I said, even if you're not there yet." He'd give her whatever time she needed, knowing that he'd do everything he could to make her fall in love with him. "I refuse to let you walk away from me—or my help—because you insist on being stubbornly independent, even if it's to your detriment. Just say yes, Emma. If not for your own sake, then for your brother's."

It may be underhanded to guilt her into moving in with him, but he didn't care. He'd use whatever was available to get his way—especially when it would be to her benefit.

"That's a low blow. You know that, right?" She shot him a glare, but didn't pull out of his arms, making him think that she might actually agree.

"We're talking about the best care—even if I have to fly him around the globe. Are you really willing to put his health and happiness on the line?" He nuzzled her as his hands drifted down to her bare ass, pulling her to him and pressing his hard cock against her, searching her out. "I swear I'll make you happy, Emma."

"Quinn…" She took a deep breath that she let out in a weary sigh. "I need some time to think about it, especially since you want me to move in with you. And so you know, I'm not a good housemate. I hog the blanket, eat your leftovers, and I'm anal about keeping the kitchen mess-free."

He had to laugh, and though she was deadly serious, he could already tell that he'd won this fight. "Sweetheart, I'll have you to keep me warm, there are *never* any leftovers, and I promise to clean my messes."

She scowled at him. "I bet you think you're funny."

"Tell you what—you've got the next few days off, right? How about we spend them together as a trial period? You can grab some of your stuff, and spend the next few days here, before you make your decision." When she frowned and looked like she was running through a mental checklist, he knew she likely used her days off to take care of restaurant stuff. "In the meantime, you can send my accountant your files, and he'll take care of payroll, your finances… whatever it is you need taken care of—and I'm not taking no for an answer."

"You're a bully. You know that, right?"

He shrugged and kissed the tip of her nose, with a sly smile. "Call me what you want, sweetheart. As long as I get my way."

"Quinn…" Her mood suddenly turned far more serious. Her brow furrowed and her hazel eyes darkened, making him want to keep the outside world at bay where nothing could bother them. "What the hell happened with Capaldi? I don't like him, and I sure as hell don't trust him to be reasonable."

Recalling Capaldi's words, Quinn's anger flared, his body tense with adrenaline. "All you need to know is that I won't let you come to harm, Emma. Not ever."

Emma led the way up the stairs to her second-story apartment, the wood underfoot creaking with age. Despite the sunny day outside, the lone window in the stairwell and the dim bulb hanging overhead did little to push back the darkness, yet another reminder that this place wasn't safe for her. Quinn had insisted on accompanying her to gather a bag of her things, though she'd surprised him by not giving him much of a fight over it.

He stood behind her, towering over her petite frame as she dug out her keys and started fumbling with the lock. "Actually, it's probably a good thing you'll be living with me, since my construction crew is scheduled to start renovations on this place first thing Monday morning."

She glared at him over her shoulder, as she gave the handle a jiggle and then shoved her shoulder into the door with expert precision, so it swung open to allow them admittance. "Don't even get me started on you buying this place. I swear, Quinn, I've never seen a person so determined to get his way."

He couldn't help but laugh as he followed her into her apartment. "You can't hold it against me, kitten. It's why I've been so successful."

Quinn took a look around—not that it took him long, given the small size of the place. And yet, it was far more cheerful than he'd expected. "This is nice, Emma. Small, but nice."

Everything but the bathroom was located in the one room, including a small kitchenette, and her bed. But a robin's egg blue adorned the walls, while butter-yellow accents lent the space a French country charm, and there were several large windows that brightened the place. To make the most of the limited floor space available to her, she'd gone vertical towards the tall ceilings with shelves and bookcases, and from what he could tell, everything served a dual purpose or had hidden storage. Even her bed was a loft, so that she could squeeze a sofa underneath.

Emma went to her closet and quickly packed a bag of clothes and personals, while Quinn wandered over to where she'd set out some pictures on a shelf, arranged artfully in a variety of white frames. He spotted one of Emma and her brother with a beautiful older woman, who could only be their mother, given that Emma looked so much like her with her refined cheekbones and full lips. There were several more pictures of people he didn't recognize, and some of Emma and Nate when they were younger. But there were also several pictures of her with Jake—pictures of them with her in his arms.

Even though Quinn didn't know the extent of their relationship, he was sure it was all in the past. And that meant he'd have to do his damnedest to keep his jealousy in check.

When she slipped her arms around his waist, he knew he'd been caught—especially when she went up onto the tips of her toes to kiss his cheek. "We're just friends."

"But you've been more. That much is obvious." He took another look at Emma smiling for the camera with her arms around Jake as he held her back. And damn, but the way Jake looked at *her*—not at the camera—left no doubt in his mind that Jake was in love with her.

"We've never hooked up, Quinn. I love him, but I don't think of him that way. He's my best friend, and we've been working together from the start, but that's it." She leaned into him and kissed him sweetly as she reached down to stroke his hard-on through his jeans. "You have no reason to be jealous, Quinn."

"Well, it's clear he's always wanted more, Emma…and that hasn't changed one bit. I can see it in the way he looks at you. And the thought of you in his arms…" He kissed her, his lips hard against hers, desperate to claim her as his own once more. He groaned against her lips when she grabbed his cock, stroking him as she distracted him from his jealousy. "Keep that up, sweetheart, and I'm going to have you on your knees with my cock in your mouth, in full view of any neighbors who might happen to look this way."

"Fuck, Quinn…why the hell does that make me so wet?" She bit his neck and stroked him harder, grabbing his cock through the worn fabric of his jeans.

He had to laugh to keep from ravaging her. "I love it that you swear when you get turned on. Like you just can't help yourself."

"I know…it's such a bad habit. But I've worked in a kitchen all my life, surrounded by men who swear a hell of a lot more than I do." She undid the button on his jeans and then slipped the zipper down, still talking between kisses and bites that had him sucking in his breath. "And you make it so I can't think straight."

"Well, my language isn't any better after years on construction sites." When she freed his cock and slipped her fingers down his hard length, he could take little more, his words coming out strained as he tried to hold back. "On your knees, Emma. Now."

The sight of her dropping before him, eager to suck him off, was more than he could bear. He sunk his fingers into her hair, fisting it, to hold her back, even as shifted forward to take him. *"Quinn...please."*

"I'm the one in control, sweetheart. Are we clear?" And the fact that she seemed to enjoy it when he took charge had him going even harder. So hard he fucking ached for her.

She gave him a playful glare. "You're such a pain in the ass, Quinn."

"That can be arranged too, kitten." He couldn't help the mischievous grin that kicked up on his lips, loving how her eyes went just a little wide and a blush crept across her cheeks.

He loosened his hold just enough to let her take him as his hips slowly thrust past those pretty pink lips of hers. Her mouth was so warm and willing, he couldn't help but quicken his pace just a little, especially when she flicked her tongue along his length and gently sucked him with a slow, purposeful rhythm.

It was impossible for him to look away from her as she took him, watching as his cock disappeared into that luscious little mouth of hers. And when she moaned with need, the vibrations of it against his cock nearly had him coming. Though his hand was still fisted in her hair, he was too far gone to do anything but let her set the pace as she worked her way up and down his cock.

"You're gorgeous, Emma. Even more gorgeous with your lips stretched around my cock." She was taking all of him...so deep...he couldn't take much more. "Fuck, sweetheart...I'm going to come."

Instead of pulling away, she gripped the back of his thighs and quickened her pace, until she pushed him over the edge and he groaned in his release, pulsing his hot cum down her throat as she swallowed it greedily, his breathing ragged and his heart racing.

And in that moment, he knew, without a doubt, that there could be no one else for him.

13

A FTER ALL THEIR LOVEMAKING, EMMA was pleasantly sore,
despite the plush seats of Quinn's car. And yet the slight dis-
comfort only spurred on her need for more. Despite being
single for most of her life, she'd always had a healthy enough sex
drive, and Quinn seemed to have kicked it into overdrive, so that
she could think of nothing but him taking her again. It left her with
a sort of euphoria she'd never experienced before, as if her body had
come alive for the first time.

"Where are we going?" Once Quinn had finally convinced her
to hand things over to his accountant so she could relax for the day,
instead of dealing with payroll and writing checks to her suppliers,
he'd decided they should take a day trip.

"I'm taking us on a bit of a detour. I wanted to check up on a
project of mine. Make sure they don't need anything and things are
progressing according to plan. After that, we can go wherever you'd
like—Paris, London, New York, San Francisco... I've got a private
jet that can take us anywhere, sweetheart." The smile he gave her
would have her agreeing to any location as long as there was a bed
with Quinn naked in it—and even then, she didn't need the bed.

"You're crazy, Quinn—but very sweet." She ran a hand down his arm, needing some sort of physical connection, even though he was focused on driving. "I'm a simple girl. I don't need you to spoil me with jets to foreign lands and house makeovers. I'm happy just to be with you."

"I like the way that sounds, love—though I'm still going to spoil you, whether you want me to or not." He glanced over in her direction, his lips kicking up at the corner, while the sun caught the green in his eyes so they sparkled like dew on spring grass. "Here we are."

The sign warmed her heart, and if this was Quinn's project, she liked him all the more. It also went a long way in explaining why he had so many dogs, and why they were so varied. "*Lucky Dog Shelter.* Did you build this?"

He turned down the long drive that led to a large building with several fenced-off areas. "I helped a little, but they had already done an amazing job at raising the money they'd need to expand. Though we don't have any kill shelters in this area, there are still plenty of states that do, and they're overrun with animals that need help. Lucky Dog works with those shelters and other volunteers to find animals whose time's run out, and bring them here so they get a second chance."

"Kind of like the chance to escape the life you grew up in?" Emma had to wonder. He'd come from so little and had accomplished so much—no easy feat, especially in today's economy.

He killed the engine and shifted in his seat to face her, his gaze lingering absentmindedly on the keys in his hands. "I had this job while trying to get through college, and I was lucky enough that someone took an interest in me and gave me a chance I'd never have gotten otherwise. I was already studying business, but a guy called Pierce Langston took me under his wing, since his own children had little interest, and gave me the sort of education and opportunities that made me who I am today. Even helped fund my first venture. My life would be completely different if it weren't for him."

Even Emma had heard of Pierce Langston, a well-known en-trepreneur and self-made billionaire. It also explained how Quinn was able to accomplish so much at such an early age. Not that he wouldn't have managed it on his own, but having such a powerhouse in business to mentor him certainly helped.

"And you, in turn, find ways to give back." The one thing she was quickly realizing was that Quinn was a generous person, and she could only imagine the sorts of things he quietly funded. Hell, even she and Nate were currently his charity case, though she was sure he didn't see it that way.

"Come on, love. I think they have a lot going on this weekend, and I want to make sure they have all the help they need."

They didn't.

They had just received a large group of animals from several kill shelters down South, and were trying to get them any medical attention they might need. Afterwards, they'd be washed and groomed, since many were in need of flea baths, and had matted fur that needed to be taken care of.

Though Quinn's presence there had stirred up all sorts of excitement, it became clear that they could use all the help they could get, given that they were trying to process over sixty animals. "Could you use some extra hands, Marlene? I can make a few calls and have people here within the hour. And for future runs, I'm happy to fund extra part-time staff if it'll help things run more smoothly."

Marlene, a kind woman in her fifties and clearly the one in charge, laid her hand on his arm, her eyes shimmering with emotion. "You're a good man—and I wouldn't say no to more help, since these poor animals have been through a lot and I'd like to get them settled after such a long drive."

Quinn nodded, and then pulled Emma aside. "I just need to phone a few people and then we can get going."

"We should stay and help. It's not as though we have anywhere to be, right?" She loved animals, and could only imagine how scared they must be after being on the road for days. In addition, if she had any hope of finding a real and meaningful relationship with Quinn, then it couldn't be about jetting off to Paris or London, or him buying her things. This would allow her to see yet another side of him, even if she already felt like she'd really gotten to know him over the last week, shattering all her misconceptions of him.

"Are you sure?" He cupped her face and stole a kiss, pulling her close. "I wanted to spoil you with some extravagant day out. Instead, we'll be up to our elbows in flea dip."

"I'm positive. Besides, I don't do well with extravagance." She loved how intense his gaze could be when he looked at her.

Once more, she had to wonder how she managed to fall for him so quickly. And though it wasn't the first time she'd had that thought, it was the first time it didn't send her into a panic.

"Let me call in the cavalry, then."

It didn't take them long to show up, and there must have been a dozen people. Emma recognized a few people, like the secretary and assistant she'd met that first day at Quinn's office. But what she hadn't expected was for Quinn's brother to show up.

Emma's heart jumped and rattled inside her chest, nowhere near ready to meet any member of Quinn's family. Before she could escape, Quinn was at her side, twining his fingers with hers, his mouth at her ear. "Don't look so nervous, sweetheart. Gabe will love you— and at least you don't have to also deal with Morgan, who couldn't make it, and Maddie, who's working out of our London office."

"Well, that's something at least, though I still highly doubt your brother will be crazy about us being together." Not when Quinn was stinking rich, and he'd only ever dated women who wanted him for his money.

"You worry too much, sweetheart." With a hand at the small of her back, he made the introductions. "Emma, this is Gabe. Gabe, Emma—the owner of the fine establishment where we had dinner the other night."

"It's a pleasure to meet you." Emma shook his hand and managed a smile, though when Gabe gave her a bit of a knowing look, she didn't quite understand it.

"The Old Port, right? On Rush Street? Great food." Unlike the green of Quinn's eyes, Gabe's were a striking blue, but the intelligence behind them was the same. "So you're local to Portmore, then?"

"I've been living in town for several years now. It feels like home, more than any other place ever has." When his gaze flicked over to Quinn with a smug look, it occurred to her that Gabe was likely the brother Quinn mentioned as the one dealing with the building she lived in. Which meant there was a very good chance he thought she was dating Quinn because she wanted something.

Perfect.

Quinn saved her. "Come on…there's plenty of work to get done. Gabe, just check in with Marlene over there."

Before long, Gabe was washing dogs, and she and Quinn were assigned towel duty on the opposite end of the room, which essentially entailed taking a sopping wet dog and attempting to dry it off. Except that the pups usually decided it'd be quicker if they lent a hand and gave themselves a good shake, spraying everyone in wet dog water. It felt like there'd been an endless stream of dogs, which at least allowed her to keep busy, though now that they were nearing the end, her worries finally got the better of her.

Quinn bumped her with his shoulder, gently toweling off a scruffy terrier, while she worked on its sister. "Don't let Gabe bother you. He's never been too fond of the women I normally date, but he'll come around once he realizes you're nothing like them."

"He's still going to lump me in with the women you're normally with, and it really bothers me that he thinks I'm only with you for your money. Which is also why you have to stop doing things for me, like fixing my building and my fridge." And when it came down to it, how different had she been, when she'd originally agreed to date Quinn in exchange for her lease?

"We're a close family and we're protective of one another—just like your brother would have happily decked me, given half a chance. But my family will be fine once they realize that this isn't some shallow relationship based on money and sex." He glanced over at her, and grabbed another towel. "Both my family and yours will come around, kitten. Because you're not going anywhere—and neither am I."

She wasn't sure she believed that either, though more and more, she found herself hoping that it was true. Once she'd tossed out all

her misconceptions of him, it turned out he was damn near perfect—even if he was stubborn and overly protective of her. Yet, what
were the chances that this could actually work out?

With both their dogs dry, he grabbed them and headed them over
to the next room, where they'd be given a final checkup, and assigned to a kennel. So it figured that with Quinn gone, Gabe would
show up with a giant wet dog and a smile on his face, though Emma
was still having a hard time deciphering the looks he was giving her.
"Here you go."

"Thanks. He's gorgeous, isn't he?" Emma gave the giant black
and white mutt a big scratch, but when she took the dog's leash from
Gabe, he grabbed her hand and held it tight, his smile suddenly
absent. She tried to pull free of his grasp, but he wasn't letting go.
"What the hell?"

"I can see why Quinn's so taken with you, but let me make something clear. He's my brother, and if you think I'm going to let you
take advantage of his generosity or break his heart, then you can guess
again." He backed her against the stainless-steel grooming table, his
muscular body threatening as he trapped her with an arm on either
side of her body. "I know your kind, and this ends now. Are we clear?"

She bit back her curses. "You know *nothing* about me." She shoved
him, though he barely budged—until a deep rumble sounded.

The dog she was supposed to be drying did *not* like how this was
all going down, and had decided Emma was in need of some help.
He was some sort of Great Dane and Newfoundland mix, which
meant he was huge—and not very happy, his angry stare focused
directly on Gabe.

Gabe was smart enough to back away from Emma, his gaze
pinned on the dog. "This isn't over, Emma. Not if you decide to
stick around."

"If you have a problem with me, then I recommend taking it up
with your brother, who, last I checked, was an adult and could make
his own decisions." She watched him stalk out of the room, cursing
up a storm, and she had to wonder if he'd left entirely.

She bent down to pet her protector, his tail wagging with a loud thump against the hard floor. "Thanks for that."

Big brown eyes looked back at her—eyes that looked wise, and yet at the same time, eyes that had experienced too much pain. Even though he was large, he was far too thin, his hip bones and ribs showing. And then there were the scars. She grabbed a dry towel and started to slowly dry him, hoping he'd finally find some happiness and love with a family who'd care for him.

When Quinn came in, it sent her protector on high alert with a low reverberating growl. "It's okay. This is Quinn." She ran a hand over his head and pet him until his growling stopped.

"Wow. He's big—and protective." Quinn carefully put out his hand to be sniffed, before cautiously petting the dog. "Does he have a name?"

She checked the tag on the dog's collar. "Says here his name is Thor. I can see why."

Quinn looked around. "Where did Gabe take off to?"

Emma wanted to groan. The last thing she wanted was to start trouble between Quinn and his brother. "I think he's gone."

With an astute gaze that bore right through her, Quinn took her in. "Did he say something to you?"

"Not much." Towel in hand, Emma distracted herself with drying Thor in a futile attempt to avoid telling Quinn what happened.

"Emma...you're lying to me—or at the very least skirting the truth—and I'm really not happy about that." He took the towel from her hand, and gently pulled her to him, wrapping her in his arms. "It's not as though I don't know what he's like."

They were both soaked to varying degrees from dealing with the dogs, so that when he held her to him, she got the initial shock of cold before the heat of his body permeated through to hers. "What do you want me to say? He acted just like any protective sibling would. It's not like you haven't given him reason to worry, when you combine buying my building with your history of dating money-hungry women."

"It doesn't matter. He still can't treat you like that, and I'm going to make damn sure he knows it." With her still in his arms, she could feel his muscles tense, his anger running just below the surface. Though the last thing she wanted was to cause problems between Quinn and his family, she thought it sweet that he'd defend her, even if it might mean rocking the boat with his family.

"How about you help me dry off Thor instead? I think he might be one of the last ones." Emma was already having visions of snuggling up to Quinn as they soaked in his massive tub.

Quinn took a look at the pup. "You know...I think he's grown rather attached to you."

And it seemed to be true. Thor was looking up at her expectantly, making her feel guilty that she couldn't take him home. She reached over and gave him a good scratch. "I wish I could take you home, but my place is too tiny."

"You forget, sweetheart. You're now living with me. And I think another dog—especially one that's already so dedicated to you— could be a good thing." He picked up the towel and finished drying off Thor, the dog's tail wagging like mad.

"Quinn...I'm only living with you temporarily. Remember? Until my apartment can be renovated." The man was going to drive her insane. "As big as he is, he'd be miserable in my studio apartment."

He gave her a cocky smile over his shoulder, which sent a rush of heat through her. "Firstly, those apartments won't be studios by the time I'm done, and besides, if I get my way—and we both know I will—you'll be living with me permanently."

The man was infuriatingly stubborn. "You're a pain in the ass, Quinn Ryker. You're just lucky..." *I love you.*

Crap. She may have cut off the words before they made it out of her mouth, but the thought had been there and there was no turning back from it.

What the hell was she going to do?

14

"SEE? I TOLD YOU THEY'D get along just fine." Quinn had done his best to reassure Emma that his dogs and Thor would get along fine together. Once all the dogs had gotten all their sniffing out of the way, Thor was quickly taken into the pack, though he only strayed from Emma's side long enough to get some food and water.

"I don't know about you, but I'm wet, stinky, and starving." She pulled her t-shirt away from her body to keep it from clinging to her, but all it took was to see that little bit of toned midriff and he could think of little else but getting her naked.

"Let's take a quick shower, and order in some pizza. Maybe watch a movie? You know…normal living together stuff." He just couldn't help himself. But the more she heard it, the more she'd get used to the idea of living with him. There'd be no letting her go now. Not when he'd fallen for her. He couldn't possibly go back to the sort of life he'd once been living.

The mere thought of her not in his arms, not in his life, left him feeling like a shard of glass had wedged its way into his heart so that even taking a breath seemed an impossible feat. And yet with her at his side, he felt newly reborn, like he could take on the world.

"Actually, that sounds perfect." She ran her hand over Thor's head with long, gentle strokes. "I'll be right back, okay?"

Watching her with her dog—and with his own—only made him like her all the more, if that were even possible. He didn't often bring women to his home, usually opting for a hotel or his apartment in town, but every now and then, they'd swing by the house for one reason or another, and his dates almost always had the same reaction. Though they were always impressed by the house itself, most of them wanted nothing to do with the dogs. And spending the day volunteering to help wash over sixty dogs? Well, that would have *never* happened.

And it was something so simple, like watching her interact with his pets, in his home, that solidified what she meant to him. He could see a future with her—the sort of future that he'd never given any thought to: one with someone he loved at his side, starting a family, and growing old together. It surprised the hell out of him, but the truth was that he could no longer imagine his life without her in it.

Wanting her more than he could have ever thought possible, they quickly stripped off each other's clothes and, after a quick adjustment to get the temperature right, he led her into the large walk-in shower, her body slipping against his as the water fell over them in a hot spray. He buried his hands in her hair, and pulled her face to his for a kiss he'd happily lose himself in for an eternity, nipping, kissing, his tongue finding hers as she reached down to stroke his cock.

He groaned into her mouth, her touch addictive and already so familiar. "Do you know how hard it was to keep my hands off you all day long? Nearly impossible."

She nipped at his neck, his ear, her words coming out on a needy breath that left him dizzy with the want of her. "Does this mean you're going to make up for lost time?"

"Such a naughty little nymph. Would you like that, kitten?" The fact that she was so willing to play these games—and get so much pleasure from them—turned him on to no end. She wasn't just going through the motions to try to please him. She genuinely enjoyed it all.

"More than anything." She continued to stroke him with one hand, her pace quickening as they discussed the matter, while her other hand reached down to heft his balls and stroke the delicate spot behind them.

"Fuck, Emma…that feels good." Too good. And it left him tempted to prolong the experience by not letting either of them come until the end of the night. Grabbing her wrists, he ignored her protests, spinning her around and pressing her hands to the wall, kicking her legs apart so that she was forced to lean forward.

Fuck, the woman was gorgeous. She had curves despite a slender waist, and a plump ass that made him want to sink his teeth in. With the water pouring over them, he ran a hand down her spine, loving how her body shimmied and arched in response.

Unable to resist, he sunk his cock into her tight, slippery pussy, hard and deep, before pulling out fully, and then did it again, eliciting curses and moans from that sweet mouth of hers. "Quinn… you're killing me. Please, just fuck me."

"Like this?" Again, he plunged in with one deep stroke, before pulling out, his need for her an almost painful ache. She ground and shifted her hips against him, searching him out, when he fisted her hair and pulled her head back, his mouth by her ear as he nuzzled her, his stubble rough against her delicate skin. "Touch yourself, sweetheart—but don't you dare make yourself come."

He lowered one of her hands between her legs and guided her fingers over her clit before letting her take over, her breath coming in ragged gasps. "I can't do this and not come, Quinn. Not when you already have me so close."

He buried his cock again—once, twice—before pulling out, her cries of frustration only adding to his need for her. "Don't come, kitten—or there'll be consequences."

This time, he left the head of his cock lingering at her slick opening, but a firm hand on her hips kept her from taking him any further. Her fingers were still gliding over her clit, her breathing now coming in strained and ragged gasps. "Fuck, Quinn...I don't think I can hold back."

When he buried himself deep inside her, he felt her body tighten around him, crying out as she came. He had to smile. "Sweetness... you weren't supposed to do that. But you like being naughty, don't you? And it makes me wonder if you'll like it just as much when I punish you."

"Why the hell does it turn me on when you talk like that?" With him still inside her, she tried moving her hips along his length, and damn, but he couldn't resist her any longer.

He pulled out of her and slapped her ass hard enough to leave a handprint against her porcelain skin, eliciting a surprised cry as she looked over her shoulder at him. She gave him a sultry smile filled with humor. "*Bastard.*"

He had to laugh. "Am I, now?"

She bit her lip, and arched her back, so her plump ass teased him enticingly. "Do it again, Quinn. *Please...?*"

He nearly groaned with his need for her, her words nearly doing him in. "Sweetheart, you're just so fucking naughty."

He ran his hand over one ass cheek and then the other, her skin warm where he'd already slapped her. Such a fine ass...and it was his. All his. He let his hand fall across the opposite cheek with a stinging slap, as she buried her head against the crook of her elbow with a wanton moan.

"*Quinn...*"

The need in her voice nearly had him coming undone. He slapped her ass once more and then plunged deep inside her with a hard thrust. She gasped and shivered in response, her hips shifting against his cock as he fisted her hair and pulled her head back, pinning her against the cold tile wall so she couldn't move her hips. "Next time, you'll do as you're told, sweetheart, or the consequences will be far greater. Do you understand?"

"Fuck..." She closed her eyes, her breath coming in shallow gasps. "Why does that make me want to misbehave?"

Her admission had him going so hard, he was dizzy with his need for her. Never before had he felt this way. Never. "Sweet girl…you're such a dirty little thing. I bet you never even knew you had it in you."

"Please, Quinn…I need you to fuck me. I need you to make me come." He could hear the tension in her voice, could feel her body squeezing around his cock, still desperate for more, despite having just come.

The aching pressure made it so he could think of nothing but taking her—and he did just that, pounding into her one hard thrust after another, taking her roughly against the shower wall, his body pressed against hers as he bit her neck.

Her body tightened once more as she cried out, coming again as he erupted inside her, his cock pulsing as he joined her with his own release, collapsing against her. Holding her to him, he tried to slow his breathing, suddenly feeling overwhelmed as his physical state ramped up his emotions. "Fuck, Emma…I'm in love with you."

There was no point in skirting the truth. Not when he was in so deep, his feelings undeniable. He wanted her and all she had to offer, and he refused to back away from how he felt.

She spun around to face him, but what he hadn't expected to see on her pretty face was a look of anger. "Damn it, Quinn… Why did you have to ruin an amazing night by screwing with my head? It's cruel to say shit like that when I'm just some passing fancy because you're bored with your usual fare."

He should be pissed off that she'd think that of him, and yet given his past, he couldn't blame her for being leery of him making those sorts of confessions.

"You know I wouldn't lie to you, Emma—and certainly not about something so serious. When I say that I love you, I mean it." He cupped her cheek and stole a kiss, while a smile tugged at his lips. "And it doesn't matter if you're not there yet, because I'm not going anywhere. Take all the time you need, love."

"You already know that I've fallen for you—hard. But I swear, if you break my heart, Quinn, I'll fricassee your balls and serve them to you for dinner."

He couldn't help but laugh. "Yes, Chef."

She looked up at him with such a look of worry, but took a deep breath, as if deciding to trust him in this last way. "I do love you, Quinn."

He let out a breath he hadn't realized he was holding, pulling her into his arms, and holding her close, his heart racing like a freight train. "I love you too, Emma. More than life itself."

☙━━❧❧❧━━❧

It had to be nearly three in the morning when Emma's cell phone went off. She grabbed it and headed into the bathroom as Quinn fought through the sleep clouding his head, though it didn't take long for her to return and start throwing on clothes. "What's going on?"

"The alarm went off at the restaurant, so the security company called me. Probably nothing. It happens. Go back to bed." When she leaned over and kissed him, he grabbed her hand.

"Give me a minute and I'll come with you." When he started to sit up, she pushed him back into bed.

"Stay…keep the bed warm for me. I swear I won't be long."

"Doesn't matter, since I'm still coming with you. It's late, it's dark, and you don't know if there's something going on at the restaurant. I refuse to have you walk in on some robbery in progress and get yourself hurt." Or worse. The thought of something happening to her was unbearable, kicking his adrenaline into overdrive.

It didn't take long before he was driving them into town, but he was feeling distracted. He swore he'd do everything he could to make sure he kept her safe, especially after Capaldi's threat. "Promise me you'll stay away from Capaldi. And if he ever shows up, you're to call me immediately."

"What happened that night? Why were the two of you fighting? You never said." She glanced over at him with her brow furrowed.

"He was talking shit, to try to piss me off, and he did just that. He got what he deserved. But that'll be nothing compared to what'll happen to him if he lays a single finger on you." Capaldi's words weaseled their way back into Quinn's thoughts, taunting and teasing him. The thought of that slimy bastard touching Emma was enough to have him contemplating murder.

"Are you saying he threatened me? Because the guy who fixed the walk-in said the damage had been done on purpose. And there've been other incidents, though we half-thought they'd just been accidents or carelessness."

"What sort of incidents? Were you hurt?" Quinn's blood was boiling with rage. He wanted to tear Capaldi limb from limb. It was one thing for him to go after Quinn, but Emma was off-limits.

"No. Just stuff with the restaurant. I'd been putting it down to rotten luck until I was told that the fridge had been tampered with, and since Capaldi has made it clear from the start that he wasn't happy I'd opened my restaurant so close to his..." She shrugged, looking worried. "What did he say?"

"He was rude and vulgar." And now Quinn was wondering if this was far more serious than Capaldi just trying to get a rise from him.

"And you punched him for it? That was awfully chivalrous, Quinn." She reached over and squeezed his hand with a worried smile.

"I protect what's mine, Emma, and make no mistake, you *are* mine." And if Capaldi already had her in his sights, then Quinn would just have to make sure Emma was protected—whether she knew it or not. "Don't blow this off. If Capaldi's behind these accidents, then this isn't something to take lightly." He brushed the hair from her eyes and leaned over to kiss her, keeping one eye on the road.

"I won't. I promise. But it's late and I just want to check on the Old Port and then crawl back into bed with you. It's my last day off and I want to make the most of it." She ran her fingers through his hair, as he turned them away from the coastline and towards the center of town. "Crap. It totally escaped me that you probably don't have tomorrow off. Sorry...I can head home when you take off in the morning."

"I took the day off since I didn't have any meetings of importance, but even if I did have to go into work, my place is now your home.

Remember? We're living together, darling." He twined her fingers with hers and brought her hand to his lips, loving the fact that they were now living together. "We should move your stuff in later today. Once you have your things with you, it'll feel more like home."

"You do realize that your house is nothing like any of the places I've ever lived in, right?"

"Don't worry, kitten. By the time I'm done fucking you in every room and on every surface, it'll feel just like home." His mind was already there—when sirens and bright flashing lights distracted him.

A horrible sinking feeling overcame Quinn, his worst fears coming true as they pulled down the road where her restaurant was located. Flames could be seen pushing against the black of night as firefighters ran towards the building—his building and her restaurant—to put out the fire.

And above it all, were Emma's heartwrenching cries as all her dreams and hard work went up in an inferno.

15

A LREADY OUT OF THE CAR, Emma tried to break free of Quinn's grasp as he held her to him, her heart shattered by the loss and devastation. Everything she was, all her hopes and dreams, were tied to the Old Port, and it was all going up in flames. Tears streamed down her face as she stopped her struggles, and instead, resorted to sobbing in Quinn's arms.

"We'll rebuild it, Emma. I promise. And whoever did this to you will fucking pay. I swear, love, I won't rest until then." His entire body reverberated with anger as he held onto her.

"Your building—and your project. I'm so sorry, Quinn." It was a huge loss for both of them, and yet somehow, knowing she wasn't alone in all this helped.

"If Capaldi is behind this, then I'm going to fucking murder the bastard." He huffed out one ragged breath after another, nestling her against his shoulder as she wept. "What's most important is that we're both safe and there shouldn't have been anyone in the building, given the late hour. We still have each other, love, and that means we can get through anything."

She nodded, hoping he was right, squeezing her eyes shut against flashing lights. Smoke and steam filled the air as the firefighters pushed back the flames, and ash drifted down like the first snow of winter. The police and fire department had questions for her, and somehow, with Quinn's help, she managed to get through them all—no, they hadn't been open for service that day and no, there hadn't been anyone at the restaurant; yes, everything was up to code and she had a sprinkler system in place; yes, she did know of someone who'd wish her ill.

By the time they wrapped things up, the sky was shifting towards dawn. Quinn pulled her into his arms and kissed the top of her head, though she felt completely numb, as if she were floating outside her body.

"Will they let us go in to see how bad the damage is?" Not knowing the extent of the damage to her restaurant was killing her. She'd seen the flames at the front of the dining room, but was hoping it'd somehow stayed contained, that she'd manage to salvage something…anything.

When she looked up at him in question, he cupped her cheek, his brows drawn over darkened eyes. "I'm sorry, love, but no. They're still investigating and it may not be safe. But eventually, they'll give us the okay—and no matter what we encounter, we'll deal with it. We'll get it all back, better than new. You have my word. Let's go home, love. It's been a long night."

With a final glance at the burnt-out shell that once housed her dreams, Quinn drove them home.

☙ ❧

Emma had barely managed a few hours of sleep when Jake showed up at Quinn's home after hearing about the fire on the local news and calling her cell. The moment Quinn opened the door, Jake crossed to her side and pulled her into a tight hug, holding her to him as the dogs circled, sniffing curiously and wagging their tails. "Em…I was so worried about you."

The familiar feel of him and the emotion in his voice set off her waterworks again, even though she didn't think she had a single tear left in her. Somehow she found the strength to pull away and dry her eyes. "We don't know how bad the damage is yet."

Quinn stepped to her side, possessiveness in the gesture. "There were sprinklers in the building, but with the fire still raging, I'm starting to wonder if some sort of accelerant had been used. Emma mentioned there've been other incidents."

Jake gave the dogs a scratch, and then stuffed his hands in his jean pockets, his gaze shifting from her to Quinn. "Yeah. But small things. Nothing like this."

"Jake...I don't know how long it'll take to get back up and running. If you have to go elsewhere for work, I'll understand." She couldn't swallow down the lump that lodged itself in her throat. After so many years of working together, the thought of cooking without him at her side was inconceivable to her, and yet she couldn't expect him to stick around.

"Don't go worrying about me, Em. I'll manage just fine, okay? Besides, I can't imagine cooking anywhere else. And if you need anything...I can help." He started to shift towards her like he wanted to pull her into his arms, but with Quinn at her side, he hesitated.

Quinn tangled his fingers with hers, though it was Jake he was addressing when he spoke. "Finn Scott will be re-opening his own place soon. If you'd like, I can see about getting you a job there until the Old Port is back up and running."

"Yeah, maybe. Just to keep me busy. I appreciate it." Emma could tell that Jake hadn't been expecting Quinn to help. And yet the way his gaze shifted from her to Quinn, it was clear he still didn't like the thought of her dating Quinn. "I'm going to get going. Keep me updated, Em. And if you need anything at all, call."

"I'll see you out." She gave Quinn's hand a squeeze and then let it go, heading out the door behind Jake, with Thor tagging along as they stepped out into a bright sunny day.

"Who's this guy?" Jake leaned against his car and gave her dog a good scratch behind the ears.

"Thor. He's mine, actually. We volunteered at the shelter yesterday and he decided to come home with me." Thor leaned against Jake's leg to have his back scratched. "He likes you."

"Glad to hear it, since he could probably make a meal of me. He's practically the size of your apartment though, Em."

She wanted to groan, though there was no point in avoiding the inevitable. "They're renovating my apartment building, so I've moved in with Quinn for now." Or longer...

"*Em!*" He shook his head and scowled. "Damn it... What the hell is it with you and this guy?"

"He's a hell of a lot nicer than you give him credit for. And yeah, things are moving fast between us, but he makes me happy." Jake was her best friend, and she needed him to like Quinn or she'd constantly feel torn between the two of them.

He pulled her into his arms and held her in a long hug, before letting out a big huff of breath that held a note of finality. "Then I suppose that's all that matters, though you know I'll always be here for you, no matter what."

"I know."

She saw Jake off with a wave, when an SUV pulled down the driveway. Gabe. She tried not to groan, but she had no desire to be around him after he'd stormed off yesterday at the shelter, making it all too clear what he thought of her. Thor let out a low rumble but Emma quickly shushed him.

"Hey, Emma." Gabe stopped in front of her, looking almost apologetic. "I'm really sorry to hear about the fire—and I'm sorry for being an asshole yesterday. It's just that we're a tight-knit family, and the women Quinn normally dates..." He let out a shrug and a sigh.

"Well, I'm nothing like them. I don't want Quinn's money, nor his help for that matter, though I'll be damned if I can get him to listen to me." Emma appreciated that Gabe was trying to make amends, though she had to wonder if it was because Quinn had said something to him. She was quickly realizing just how protective

Quinn was of her, and she knew he hadn't been too happy with the way Gabe had treated her, even if she hadn't told him what had happened. "I do appreciate the apology. I love your brother, and family's important."

It felt odd to make that sort of declaration out loud, and to Quinn's brother no less. But it also felt right. She loved Quinn. Without a doubt.

"Now all I have to do is get this dog to forgive me." He gave her a charming smile that reminded her of Quinn, as he put out his hand to give Thor a chance to sniff him. "I can't believe Quinn adopted him."

"Actually, he's mine." She ran a hand over her pup's big head and tried to set him at ease. "It's okay, Thor. Go on." Her encouragement was all it took for Thor to forgive Gabe.

They found Quinn in the kitchen, brewing a pot of coffee. It was a good start, but they'd yet to have breakfast after the morning's commotion, and coffee alone wasn't going to cut it.

"Why don't I cook us some breakfast? Gabe, have you eaten?" Emma let Quinn pull her close and kiss her temple, making her want to linger in his arms, his touch comforting after such a devastating night.

Gabe leaned against the counter, shifting the leather messenger bag on his shoulder. "Actually, I haven't. But...do you mind if I steal Quinn for a minute? I know you guys have been through a lot, but I've got some work stuff I have to go over with him, and I'm afraid it can't wait."

She didn't quite understand the look Gabe gave Quinn, but she let it go, too exhausted and mentally drained. "He's all yours."

Emma focused on her cooking to keep her mind from straying to her restaurant. And yet it was hard not to think of it.

Quinn's fridge was nearly as large as the one she had at her restaurant, and though it was stocked with more than enough junk food and beer, there was also plenty of fresh and healthy food for her to work with. Asparagus, farm fresh local eggs, goat cheese, bacon, chives. Perfect for an omelet.

She started her prep, though she didn't start cooking, not wanting the food to get cold if the boys were going to be awhile. Luckily, it didn't take them too much longer to wrap up whatever it was they were discussing. And yet, their mood, already somber due to the fire, had shifted to something even worse.

Something was wrong. She just didn't know what that something was.

Quickly cooking up their meal, she got everyone fed, and though they seemed to enjoy the food and declared it to be delicious, little else was said.

Emma cleaned up as Quinn saw Gabe off. Yet once Quinn returned and wrapped his arms around her waist, she couldn't help but ask. "What's wrong, Quinn?"

"Just some complications with a project. Nothing you need to worry yourself about, sweetheart. These things always sort themselves out." He cupped her face and kissed her. "About your restaurant—I'm happy to help you rebuild, since the insurance money might get tied up in red tape if it turns out to be arson."

"I hate having to ask you to loan me any money, Quinn, but… crap. I might have to. Rebuilding is going to take long enough as is, without having to wait for the insurance money to come in." She got the sinking feeling this was all going to be a nightmare to deal with. And what if they decided not to pay up? Did her policy even include arson?

"What if we moved the restaurant to a new location just around the block? I have another property that could easily be turned into a restaurant. We could have it up and running in no time at all, and your customer base would be the same since the location wouldn't really change much." His worried eyes searched her face before kissing her, though she was too distracted to enjoy herself.

"Quinn…I appreciate the offer. It's way too generous, but I can't. You're already doing far too much."

16

QUINN DIDN'T KNOW WHAT THE hell he was going to do. Gabe had *not* brought him good news. Despite the fire and Gabe's attempts to get a new set of plans passed—plans that would keep Emma's restaurant in its current location—his investors were refusing to approve the change now that the original plans had been put through.

It was why he hated working with investors—especially powerful ones. At the time, it'd seemed like a good strategy for building allies. Now? It might end up ruining the one relationship that truly mattered.

Though Emma was putting on a brave face, Quinn knew she was barely holding it together, and it was absolutely killing him, especially when he had to leave her and go to work. It'd been a few days since the fire, and she looked lost—lost and heartbroken. It didn't help that they'd yet to hear back from the arson investigator or the insurance company, which were both still compiling their reports.

Quinn looked over the plans for Rush Street again, trying to figure out a way around his problem when Gabe walked into his office and dropped himself in a chair, undoing the buttons of his suit and loosening his tie. "I'm telling you, Quinn, the only hope you have of keeping the Old Port in its current location is to find a way to get Sullivan to agree to your new set of plans. He's the one with the most to lose since he'd planned on putting his nightclub in that spot. The other investors don't care much, as long as it doesn't increase the cost or cause more delays."

Quinn knew Gabe was right. But Sullivan was a stubborn bastard and would dig his feet in just to be a pain in the ass. "I've got an appointment scheduled with him later this afternoon. We've got that property by the waterfront that's a far more valuable location, so I'm hoping I can convince him to shift his club to that location since he'd be getting a better deal."

"It's only a few blocks away, so he might go for it, though damn, Quinn. That's a huge loss, seeing that the property is waterfront and worth twice the money. And for what?" Gabe shook his head, his gaze far too judgmental.

Quinn's anger flared, knowing full well what his brother was thinking. "Don't, Gabe. Not a fucking word."

Gabe threw up his hands, easily able to read Quinn's mood. "Don't get angry with me, man. I like Emma—and I get that I was mistaken about her. But you're acting like a lovesick fool, and it's costing us money."

"I can make more money—and it's not like we don't already have enough to absorb that sort of loss. That's nothing, and you know it. But I can't lose Emma. And that's exactly what'll happen if she thinks I manipulated and lied to her." Quinn knew how it'd look— like he'd made her empty promises just to get her into his bed.

"I want you to be happy, but she's got you off your game and you know it." Gabe shook his head, missing the fact that Quinn was getting angrier by the second. "What you need is to find some tall leggy model to fuck."

Quinn grabbed his brother by the jacket and hauled him to his feet—no easy task given that his brother was as big as he was. "Get the fuck out before I do something we'll all regret."

Gabe shrugged out of his grasp and shook his head. "You know I only want what's best for you."

"Then open your fucking eyes—because what's best for me is Emma."

Quinn got nowhere with Sullivan, who was being a stubborn ass because he liked to have the upper hand on Quinn, even if it was over something petty. So much for going into the deal to make allies—one of Gabe's ideas. Well, that'd be the first and last time he'd take on other business partners. Quinn could manage just fine without them, since he certainly didn't need help funding any of his projects or investments.

As for Emma and her restaurant, he just had to convince her that the waterfront spot he'd offered Sullivan was the perfect location. He'd set it all up for her, doing his best to copy her original design on Rush Street and make it even better, no expense spared. And then, once it was perfect, he'd show it to her and explain what had happened. She'd see that he'd tried to make amends, that he hadn't meant to lie to her, but rather it was a series of unforeseen circumstances.

It had to work.

He got home to find the place smelling incredible. Not even the dogs budged from the kitchen to greet him, like they normally did. Instead they were transfixed by Emma, who no doubt had been throwing them the occasional nibble and scrap.

"You're going to spoil them." He slipped his arms around her waist, holding her to him from behind as she continued to work, his lips making their way along the slope of her neck. The fact that he could come home to her after a rotten day...he'd never had anything like that before. And though he should be absolutely terrified at the domesticity of it all, he found it actually left him with a feeling of blissful contentment.

She finished stirring the pot, adjusted the heat to a simmer, and then spun around in his arms to face him. With a sultry smile, she wrapped her arms around his neck and went up onto her toes to kiss him, her lips soft and warm against his. "You know, you're damn sexy in a suit."

"Well, get your fill, darling, because I'm giving you about another thirty seconds before I strip both of us naked so I can sprawl you out over the kitchen island and bury my face in your sweet pussy." He cupped her ass with both hands and dragged her up against him, his cock going hard as he kissed her, his tongue forcing its way past her lips, the feel of her in his arms erasing the stress of the day.

He trailed kisses down her neck, cupping her breast and running his thumb over her nipple. But when he went to pull off her t-shirt, he realized it was actually one of his old worn tees. "I love that you're wearing my clothes. That's just so fucking hot." It added to that feeling that she was his and his alone.

"Even though it was clean, it still smelled like you." She bit her bottom lip. "I missed you, Quinn. The place felt empty without you here."

"Well, I'm home now, darling." He lifted her into his arms, so her legs wrapped around his waist, his mouth on hers, greedily kissing her as she held onto him, her arms slipping around his neck. Putting her down on the large kitchen island, he stole one more kiss before turning his attention to getting her naked.

She helped him by shimmying out of her jeans as he yanked them off the rest of the way, her hands then moving to his suit jacket. He tossed it aside, but when he started loosening his tie, she stopped him with a rough kiss, her words spoken against his lips. "Leave the shirt and tie on—please?"

"Like that, is it? Does it turn you on, darling? Or maybe..." He had to smile while stealing another kiss. "Maybe it's the tie? Do you see it and think of the tie I used to bind you to my bed...making you come before fucking you roughly from behind? Is that it, my naughty little nymph?"

"Fuck, yes..." She groaned against his lips as she stroked him through the fabric of his trousers, his cock pulsing against her hand.

He yanked her lace panties off and nestled himself between her legs, running his hands up her toned thighs to tease her clit, letting his fingers run over her slick folds. "You're always so wet for me, darling. I love that about you…that you're always so eager, so willing, so needy. As if you live for me to fuck you."

"I do. Always…" She bit her bottom lip when he slipped his finger inside her, but only for a moment. With a needy moan, her eyes slid closed and her hips tilted towards him, searching him out, though he did little but tease her.

Hooking one leg and then the other over his shoulders, he opened her up to him as he buried his face between her legs, lapping at her juices and sucking on her clit as he slipped two fingers deep inside her. Slowly thrusting into her, he curled his fingers, his tongue firm against her clit. Increasing his pace, he finger-fucked her on the cool granite counter, tasting her very essence as she buried her fingers in his hair, her body tightening and undulating as he pushed her close to her orgasm. She cried out as she came, Quinn's name on her lips, though he was far from through with her.

He continued to suck and lick her sensitive clit, as she gasped and tightened her legs around his shoulders, her words coming out on thready breaths as if she couldn't quite fill her lungs with enough air. "Oh, fuck…Quinn…I just came…I can't…"

"You can and you will, darling." He nipped and sucked at her clit, stroking the swollen and fleshy bundle of nerves deep inside her as his other hand reached up to pinch her nipple through the t-shirt she was still wearing, his arm pinning her to the island as she squirmed beneath him. And then she was crying out again, her body shaking and quivering as her orgasm tore through her, her breathing heavy as Quinn trailed kisses over the flare of her hips and the curves of her belly.

He looked up at her, and damn, if she wasn't the most gorgeous thing he'd ever seen, with her cheeks all flushed. "Come on, kitten. I'm starving and want you to feed me."

She sat up and grabbed his tie, pulling him close and kissing him hard as her other hand stroked his hard cock. "But...I want you to fuck me, Quinn. Please..."

"Sweetheart, I've gotta tell you...I love it when you ask me to fuck you—but I'm still going to make you wait. Let the anticipation build through the night so that when I finally fill your sweet pussy with my cock, you'll come so hard you won't be able to string together a coherent thought."

And wait Emma did, though she had to admit, Quinn lived up to his promise—and more.

17

SITTING BY JAKE'S SIDE ON the sofa in Quinn's living room, Emma tried to swallow down her emotions as she told Jake about the fire inspector's findings. "They said that an accelerant had to have been used. It's a total loss, Jake. The kitchen, the dining room, the bar. Nothing survived."

When her tears spilled over and she choked back a sob, Jake pulled her into his arms and held her tightly to him. "Oh, Em. I'm so sorry. But we'll rebuild it, right? And we'll make it better than ever. Have you heard from the insurance company yet?"

"No. Nothing yet. And I'm starting to go stir crazy. It's only been a week since the fire and Quinn's taken some time off to be with me but he still has a business to run and he's had to go in the last few days. I need to get back to work, Jake." She'd been keeping busy by cooking up a storm for Quinn. Freshly baked bread, elaborate meals, sinful desserts. And she walked the beach, taking the dogs with her. Yet it still wasn't enough unless Quinn was with her, his distracting presence the only thing that could really keep her mind from her restaurant.

Jake sat back, though he took her hand in his, offering her a little bit of comfort. "Once you get the insurance money, you'll be able to keep yourself busy with the renovations to the restaurant. Hopefully it won't take long for them to cut the check, and then we'll be back up and running in no time at all."

"Quinn offered to loan me the money." Actually, he offered to cover the cost outright, though she couldn't let him do that.

"If you don't feel comfortable taking the money from him, I'll happily loan it to you. You know that, right?" He gave her hand a squeeze, worry lining his brow.

"I appreciate it, though I'm hoping the insurance company won't take forever." And if they did, she supposed she'd just have to borrow the money. "The cops also let me know that they'll be interviewing everyone who works at the Old Port—me included. So don't be surprised if they call you down to the station."

"I hope they'll also take a look at Capaldi. You know he wasn't happy—especially after that fight with Quinn." Jake shook his head with a sigh. "I'm assuming Quinn had good reason to deck him?"

"Capaldi was talking shit about me, which was why he didn't let it go. I know you don't care for Quinn, but he cares about me, Jake." And after her last boyfriend cheated on her and lied straight to her face, it felt good to have someone like Quinn in her life.

"I hope you're right, Em. Look…I should get going. Keep me updated, yeah?" Jake got to his feet and grabbed her hand, pulling her up to him. "And if you need anything at all, just call me."

"I will." She saw Jake off with a hug, glad he'd been able to swing by. So used to seeing him nearly every day, she'd missed not having him around.

It was nearly lunch time, and unable to bear the thought of rattling about the house bored, she decided to put together a quick lunch and take it to Quinn. He'd mentioned that he only had a few things on his plate, and she hoped it'd be a nice surprise for him, though she half-worried she might just be in the way.

Emma just wasn't used to having so much time on her hands, and though she'd brought over more of her things, it still felt like

Quinn's home, not hers. Maybe with more time, it'd start to feel like hers, too. The thought warmed her, knowing that the last few weeks with Quinn had left her falling for him fast and hard, and he made her happier than she could have ever imagined possible.

She loved him—and he loved her. And damn if that didn't make her giddy, despite all her problems.

Feeling better about things, and with the excitement of seeing Quinn thrumming through her veins like a live wire, she finished packing their lunch, and headed into town. Basket in hand, she took the elevator up, remembering the first time they met—and her meeting with Quinn afterwards. She couldn't help but smile, recalling how furious he'd made her and what a jerk she'd thought him. How mistaken she'd been.

Stepping off the elevator and into Quinn's business suite, she walked up to Nancy's desk. "Don't suppose Quinn's here? I brought him some lunch."

"I'm so sorry. He's out at the moment, but I can contact him. Let him know you're here." So much for surprising him. Emma took a seat in the waiting area but it didn't take long for Nancy to approach her. "Mr. Ryker's on his way. If you'd like to wait in his office...you'll probably be more comfortable there."

"That'd be great." Emma thanked Nancy as she was let into Quinn's office and then got busy setting out their lunch, oddly nervous with a flutter in her belly, no doubt due in part to the fact that she was doing something so personal in his work space. It was a rather public announcement that they were together, and she just hoped he wouldn't mind.

There were some papers on his desk, and though she didn't want to move his work, she didn't want to get food on it either. Still... she hated people messing around with her own stuff, and wanted to extend him the courtesy—until a set of blueprints caught her eye.

She immediately recognized the building as the one housing her restaurant, and if she'd had any doubt, the address on the corner of the plans verified it for her. The plans were impressive, and she couldn't help but get excited at the thought that her restaurant would be in such a gorgeous building—once her restaurant was rebuilt.

Sneaking a peek at the next page, she forced herself to do a double take. It felt like someone had sucker-punched her. Surely these had to be the old plans—the original ones, before Quinn renewed her lease. Because the location where her restaurant currently stood? Well, that was marked on the plans as some sort of nightclub belonging to Sullivan Investments.

She scrambled to find the date on the plans, desperate to confirm that the plans weren't recent, that her restaurant location was safe, and that Quinn hadn't betrayed her. There, next to where the plans had been approved by the city, was the date.

It couldn't be.

Tears escaped before she even fully realized that she was crying. It was as if her whole world had been tipped upside down, and she felt crushed by the weight of Quinn's betrayal, leaving her unable to take a breath until her lungs burned from it.

The date on the plans was for just over a week ago—just before the fire. He'd lied about renewing her lease. Lied about letting her keep her restaurant.

He'd lied straight to her face—about the most important thing in her life, no less.

With her heart shattered, she bolted out of Quinn's office, ignoring Nancy's worried concerns as she repeatedly hit the button for the elevator, which mercifully was still there, so she didn't have to wait.

She had to get to the lease…had to check it.

Except that she wasn't sure she could. Crazy as that night had been with Capaldi and Quinn fighting, she couldn't remember if she'd made a copy to take home with her, or if the only copy had just been burned in the fire—a fire set only days after Quinn had gotten the approval for his plans.

Did Quinn have something to do with the fire? Was it his way of getting rid of her restaurant without her being any the wiser? She couldn't help but wonder—and that nearly killed her.

18

QUINN WASN'T SURE WHAT THE hell had happened, but something had upset Nancy and she was now rambling. He caught Emma's name in the jumble of words. "Nancy, slow down and tell me what happened to Emma. Where is she?"

"She left. Everything was fine. I let her into your office, since she had several bags of food and probably wanted to get things set up for you. She couldn't have been more than five minutes when she ran out of here in tears. I tried to talk to her, but she got on the elevator before I had a chance to stop her. I'm so sorry, Mr. Ryker. I don't know what happened."

A sinking feeling overcame him as he went to his office. The plans...right there on his desk where he'd been working on them, out in plain view. He hadn't taken the time to put them away when he'd realized he was running late for his appointment.

Fuck.

"How long ago did she leave, Nancy?" He all but shook her. *"How long?"*

"I don't know. It had to be about twenty, twenty-five minutes ago. I'm so sorry. I didn't think it would be a problem to put her in your office."

Quinn was already heading for the elevator, his mind racing. Home. She'd go there. In the meantime, he pulled out his cell to call her, to try to explain. And yet, what the hell would he say? He'd screwed her over. Gone back on his promise to her. It may not have been his intention, and he may have tried to do right by her, but it didn't change the fact that her restaurant space was going to another, and it was his fault. He'd made her a promise he couldn't keep. And now, he didn't know if she'd ever forgive him.

The call went straight to voicemail. Again. And again. He drove like a maniac, shifting from one gear to the next, forcing his car to hug the curves of the road, and flying around other drivers. She had to have gone to his place. And if she hadn't, then where? Her apartment? Her brother's? Or would she go to Jake's?

He pounded the steering wheel in frustration, cursing and wanting to punch something, though he knew he had no one to blame but himself. Skidding down his drive, he was gutted with the realization that her car wasn't there. He let himself in and was greeted by all the dogs, except Thor.

His world was crashing down around him.

Her drawers had been hastily emptied, some of them barely pushed shut, as though she'd only bothered with the necessities. He had to find her. Had to explain to her.

He raced around Portmore in a daze. She wasn't at her apartment, and her friend and neighbor, Ivy, hadn't seen her. That left her brother and Jake. He groaned. Neither of those were good options, though if he had to guess, she'd likely pick Jake, since Nate lived a half hour away.

The thought of her with Jake... It took all he had not to see red, especially when it was clear Jake was in love with her and would like nothing more than to be with her. A quick call to his assistant got him Jake's address, which luckily had been listed. But he couldn't get there fast enough, though he'd yet to figure out what the hell he was going to say to her.

Quinn half-expected Jake to live in some rundown shack or tiny apartment. Instead, he found himself pulling down the drive to a nice-looking log home nestled in the woods on the other side of Portmore. *There*—next to Jake's car was Emma's.

He warred with his anger as he pounded on Jake's door, pissed off that Emma had turned to another man when she was upset. Pissed off that another man was there to comfort her—and pissed off with himself that he was the one who'd upset her.

It took Jake longer than expected to answer the door, and fuck, but he was pulling a t-shirt on and standing in the doorway, blocking his view and essentially refusing him passage. "What do you want, Ryker?"

"I need to talk to Emma." Quinn was trying to keep his anger and jealousy in check but he was barely managing it, especially when Jake was playing gatekeeper.

"Buddy...you fucked up, big time. And you have some nerve to come here looking for her after what you did." Jake shook his head and leaned against the doorjamb, stuffing his hands in his pockets. "She wants nothing to do with you—not right now, at any rate."

"Then I want to hear it from her—not you—and I'm not taking no for an answer. I'm not going anywhere until I get to speak to her." He was going to fucking lose it if he didn't get to see Emma.

Jake scoffed with a shake of his head. "That's not going to happen, so I suggest you go. If she wants to speak to you, she knows where to find you."

Thor came trotting past Jake to greet him, his tail wagging. He reached down to pet him, but his focus was on the space just beyond Jake, hoping that the reason Thor had come out was that Emma wasn't far behind. *"Emma! Please..."*

She put a hand on Jake's waist as she slipped by him, clearly still upset, her eyes red from crying. And damn, but the familiarity between her and Jake, the fact that she would so casually touch him as if she'd done it a million times, nearly killed him. "It's okay."

"Em—you don't need to talk to him if you don't want to." Jake glared at Quinn, but he took a step back when she leaned in and said something to him.

Again, the level of comfort between them made him want to go over there and punch Jake. She was his, damn it. His and his alone. He loved her…loved her more than he could have ever imagined loving anyone.

Jake gave them some privacy, but when Quinn tried to close the distance between them, she put a hand up to stop him and took a step back. "Don't, Quinn. Unless you can tell me that I'm somehow mistaken about you giving my restaurant space to someone else."

"Emma… It's not like that." He didn't care that she wanted him to stay away; he couldn't help himself. It was killing him that she was angry with him—killing him that he'd fucked things up between them. "When I promised you I'd renew your lease, I was under the impression that I still had a month to make whatever changes I wanted. I didn't realize that the signing got bumped up. I'd made you that promise thinking I could still alter the deal, but it was too late. Gabe had met with the investors and the contract was signed. I tried to get the investor to take a different space, but he wouldn't budge. I tried, love. I swear it."

Close as she was, he couldn't help but reach out and touch her, cupping her face in his hand. Her eyes closed for a moment, but then she pulled away. "Don't touch me, Quinn. Because you know what? I saw the date on those plans—and they're dated days before we made our agreement. Fuck, Quinn…you even dropped off my new lease after it'd gone through—a lease that *conveniently* went up in flames, mind you. Except that I made a copy." She pulled out a piece of paper from her back pocket and unfolded it. "I wasn't sure I had, since I was rattled by your fight with Capaldi, but there it was sitting in my purse—a copy of my lease that didn't end up as ashes."

It felt like she'd just ripped his heart out. "You don't mean…you can't actually think I had anything to do with the fire?" She couldn't possibly… He felt gutted. "Emma—I had nothing to do with it. And I swear, I tried to renegotiate the contract so you could keep your current location. I never meant to hurt you."

"But you did. You not only hurt me, but *you lied to me*, Quinn— after you swore we'd be nothing but honest with each other." Her eyes shimmered with tears as she turned to go. He grabbed her hand, but she shrugged free of his grasp, turning back to face him with tears streaming down her cheeks. "I can't do this. You made me think I could trust you—you made me fall in love with you... And don't tell me that you didn't know about the plans because my lease has a goddamned fucking loophole in it that allows you to take over my space at your discretion."

He wanted to groan. It was the final nail in his coffin. Clearly he hadn't buried that clause deep enough in the contract or wrapped it up in enough legalese. "But only if a better location is made available to you at no additional cost, with all your expenses taken care of. Emma, my brother told me about the contract going through that very day, and though I was hoping to find a way out of it, I knew that I might not be able to. At least this way, the loophole allows you the freedom to move your restaurant without incurring any expenses and without having to wait for the insurance to cough up the money."

"So you decided to cover your ass, legally. Nice, Quinn. That's really fucking nice." She swiped at her tears and looked away, as if the very sight of him was too much for her to bear in that moment. "Well, I don't want you or your fucking money."

"It wasn't like that. I swear. Just come back home, love—I'll explain everything. And I swear, I'll do everything I can to make things right between us. It's killing me to see you cry." He refused to let her go. He needed her—needed her in his life, and he'd be damned if he was going to let her walk out on him, on what they had. "*I love you, Emma.*"

"Well, you should have thought of that before you lied straight to my face. The only reason I started dating you was because of that lease—and then you made me fall for you. But you lied, Quinn. Instead of coming clean, you lied to me, after you promised never to do such a thing."

"I was trying to fix things. You need to believe me."

But she didn't. And before he had the chance to convince her otherwise, she was bolting up the steps, leaving him to call out after her.

Quinn went over the signed contract, trying to find a way out of it. There had to be a way.

"You already have our lawyers trying to find a way out of the deal, but it's not looking good. Not to mention, it's going to tarnish our reputation if you back out of this deal." Gabe shook his head with a weary sigh. "I know you like Emma—and I like her too—but, Quinn…she's just going to have to deal with it. It's not like her lease wasn't up anyway."

Quinn was so frustrated, he wanted to punch something. Wanted to go back to Jake's and drag Emma back to his house. Wanted to remind her why they were so good together.

"Her lease wasn't up, because I had already agreed to renew it, thinking I still had another month before that contract was finalized. I thought I could still make changes to it, not realizing the meeting got moved and you'd pushed forward with the deal." He ran a rough hand down his face, wanting to scream. "You don't get it, Gabe. I love her. And I've taken away the one thing that was important to her."

"*Whoa…*" Gabe threw up his hands. "I did *not* just hear that. You can't possibly be in love with her, Quinn. It's one thing to hear that sort of nonsense from her, but from you? Are you fucking kidding me? It's been like two dates or something. Have you lost your mind?"

Quinn glared at his brother and forced himself not to do something rash. "Are you sure you want to question me about that right now? 'Cause I'll give you fair warning, Gabe—I'm in no fucking mood."

"Well, whether you love her or not, it makes little difference. That space is still going to Sullivan, because that man's as stubborn and proud as you are, and he's not backing down. Not for all the money in the world." Gabe paced Quinn's office floor, looking every bit as annoyed as Quinn felt.

"That other retail space by the water…we'll move her restaurant there." It would have to work. That was all there was to it. "I'll handle this one personally. And it'll just have to blow away the original space."

Gabe looked at him like he was insane—and maybe he was, at this point. "And what if she still doesn't forgive you and take you back? Huh? What the fuck are you going to do then?"

"That's not an option."

19

"**I** DON'T WANT TO TALK ABOUT it, Jake." Emma hated crying. And yet she couldn't stop the goddamned waterworks. All because of Quinn.

She didn't know what the hell to believe anymore. It certainly could have happened as he said, though it hadn't kept him from lying to her, trying to strike one deal after another until he'd gotten her in his bed.

With his face lined with worry, Jake focused on petting Thor as if he couldn't bear to see her crying. "Do you think it was intentional on his part—telling you he'd renew the lease when he couldn't?"

"He clearly knew there were issues since he put a goddamned clause in the lease, but…I don't know. Maybe he was just hopeful that he could get things ironed out." And maybe she was a stupid fool, since she'd not only fallen for him, but was trying to make excuses for him.

"I suppose that if you hadn't found the plans, and he did manage to fix things, you'd have been none the wiser. I doubt he'd have bothered admitting to his lies." Jake shook his head, looking pissed off enough to have her thinking that it was a good thing Quinn wasn't around.

She swiped at her tears, though they kept coming. "That's what hurts the most. The entire time, he'd been talking about honesty, and how I could trust him. How he'd never lie to me or hurt me. And like a fucking fool, I believed him. One lie after another."

How could she have been so stupid? So naïve. He must have thought her such an easy target to manipulate. She felt like such an idiot. And one would think that given her past, with her ex lying and cheating his way through their whole relationship, that she'd be more cautious, more leery of handsome men making promises they had no intention of keeping. Quinn might be different than her ex, but the results were the same. She'd still had her heart trounced.

Jake ran a hand down her arm, his touch gentle and caring. "What are you going to do, Em?"

"It's not like I have many options. He even owns my apartment building at this point." How the hell was she supposed to try to get over Quinn when he'd imbedded himself in the most important parts of her life?

Jake gave her a big shrug and waved away her last concern. "You know I have plenty of room here. Move in with me. That'll be one less thing you have to worry about and I'd love to have the company."

It's not as though she had a whole lot of options at this point. "If you're sure..."

"I am. This place has far too many bedrooms, including the second master suite you're currently staying in. It's too big for it to just be me rattling around the place." He cupped her face and wiped her cheeks dry. "I'm here for you, Em. I always will be—no matter what you need. You'll get through this."

She nodded, though with her heart still shredded into a million little pieces, she didn't know how she'd get through it.

Her phone buzzed. The police department. With her heart racing, she took the call and listened as the police detective rattled through their findings. By the time she hung up, she felt even worse. "They found out who'd been sabotaging us at the restaurant. Fucking

Tony. Not only was he missing his shifts, he was the one responsible for causing us all that grief."

Jake shook his head, anger pouring off him in waves. "Are you fucking kidding me? I'm going to murder that lazy bastard. So did they arrest him?"

"Not for the fire. They don't think he was the one who set it." And that left her thinking of Capaldi again. "He said they don't have many other leads."

"If it wasn't Tony, then it has to be Capaldi."

"They're looking into it, but as of yet there's no evidence pointing in his direction."

⚯

"I don't want to go anywhere, Jake." Emma felt like an empty shell. Her restaurant, her entire purpose in life, was gone, and with Quinn's betrayal only adding to her grief, she'd never felt such heartache. She could barely muster the energy to pull herself up off Jake's sofa, Thor at her feet keeping vigil. Quinn came by every single day, though Jake never let him in, knowing it'd do nothing but upset her further.

Jake sat down on a nearby ottoman, and brushed the hair from her face, looking more worried than she could ever recall seeing him. "Come on, Em. It's been two weeks since you guys split up and you've barely left the house—not to mention Quinn looks like absolute crap. It's not that I like the guy, but I doubt the man's slept a wink or eaten a single thing since this all went down, even if he looks ready to punch me in a fit of jealousy, each and every time he sees me."

"Serves him right. Bastard." Her eyes burned as she tried to swallow down the lump in her throat.

Jake grumbled out a groan of frustration and got to his feet. "That's it. We're going out—and you don't get to say no. Not this time. We have to find a new location for the restaurant, and there's a ton of planning that needs to get done."

"The insurance company is dragging its feet while the arson investigation continues and until I get some money in, I have no funds for putting down deposits on anything." She put up a hand to stop him, knowing exactly what he was going to say. "And I can't take your money when I don't know when the hell I'll be able to pay you back."

He pulled her up off the sofa and got her standing, tossing aside the throw that clung to her. "Then consider it an investment. Let me be your business partner, Em. I got a sizeable inheritance, and though it may not be the billions Quinn's managed to rack up, I've made some nice investments, and the returns have been considerable."

Taking a deep breath, she tried to snap through the fog in her head. She knew Jake would be the perfect business partner. And maybe this was just what she needed to get herself out of her funk. "Are you sure that's what you want to do? Especially when they haven't caught whoever set the fire? Someone doesn't like me, Jake. And I doubt it'll stop until we figure out who the hell it is."

Anger darkened his brown eyes, until they'd nearly gone black. "I'm not letting anyone stop me, Em. And I sure as hell won't let them fucking intimidate us. We're going to do this, and whoever it is better get used to it."

She hadn't revisited the thought that Quinn was behind the fire. It would have been an easy way to force her to move the restaurant, and since they'd been planning a remodel anyway, it was no skin off Quinn's back. And yet, she couldn't think of him going to such extremes, especially when he knew what the Old Port meant to her, and the cops hadn't mentioned him.

Taking a deep breath, she pushed aside her emotions, and thoughts of Quinn. And though she still felt like a ghost of her former self, she managed a whisper of a smile. "I guess we're partners then."

"I think this calls for a celebration. Let's go grab some lunch and we can make plans. Find a new location that'll be even better than the first." He pulled her into his arms and gave her a big hug. "You'll be all right, Em. I'm going to make sure you pull through this."

Emma took a deep breath and let it out in a weary sigh as she rested her head on Jake's chest, hoping he was right, even as her tears threatened once more.

Q UINN NEVER SHOULD HAVE LET his brothers drag him out to
a club. He was in no mood for the lights, the noise, or the
crowds, and the sort of drinking he wanted to do was the
kind best done at home.

Morgan bumped his shoulder. "Looks like you've got an admirer.
She'll help you forget whatever's made you such a grumpy fuck
as of late."

Quinn glanced over at the leggy blonde. Pretty, tall, curvy, and
looking all too willing. She would have been a perfect distraction
before Emma. But now? What the hell was the point? He had no
interest in her, none whatsoever.

Ignoring Morgan's comment—and the blonde—he turned back
to business. "The police called to let me know that they don't believe
the fire is related to the other incidents at Emma's restaurant, and
they're starting to wonder if it's not related to Emma, but rather
Ryker Investments."

"Fuck...I can't imagine why anyone would have it in for us."
Morgan usually had his head buried in finding them new ventures
to invest in, but he seldom dealt with any of the day-to-day stuff,

preferring to do his own thing. He wasn't exactly a loner, but he certainly didn't go out of his way to deal with people.

"Unfortunately, there are always people we've pissed off. It's part of doing business, and we've certainly made our share of enemies along the way. Problem is, they're not coming up with many leads based on just the evidence from the fire, so they've got some sort of consultant or special investigator coming up from Boston." Quinn wanted this figured out.

The thought of someone threatening his family, threatening Emma, left him furious. She could have easily been at the restaurant when the fire was set, not to mention all her customers. It could have been a tragic disaster.

"At least they're staying on it." Gabe's eyes narrowed in anger as he shook his head. "A fire isn't exactly a small-scale threat, yeah? They need to find whoever's fucking with us before this escalates."

"Exactly. They're going to want to sit down with us and go over all our investments and properties, any issues we may have had with competitors." Shit, that was a long list. "Gabe, if you could meet with the investigator they're sending, I'd appreciate it, since you usually deal with all our documents and contracts, and are most familiar with those details. And since they don't know what the motivation behind the fire was or if that was the end of it, we're going to have to be diligent."

"Whatever you need, I'm here. I'll also let our foremen and property managers know. Make sure security is beefed up." Gabe took a long sip from his pint, before tilting his head back towards the blonde. "She's got a couple of friends now. One for each of us."

Quinn still had absolutely no interest in a hookup, especially with his thoughts still lingering on Emma. The thought of her in danger, that he couldn't be by her side to protect her was killing him—and he'd had enough. "I'm afraid you're going to have to manage without me. I've got a busy day ahead of me tomorrow."

Shaking his head, Gabe glared at him as Quinn got to his feet. "For fuck's sake, Quinn... Busy doing what? Working on Emma's restaurant? I get that you're in love with her—and I get that you're probably worried about her, too—but that woman has totally fucked you up. You either need to forget about her, or you need to figure out a way to win her back—one that'll be quicker than building her a goddamned restaurant."

"Don't you think I've tried, Gabe? What the fuck?" Ready to punch someone, he grabbed his jacket and got ready to go. "Just mind your own damn business if you don't have anything constructive to say."

"Quinn…for fuck's sake. *Stay*."

But he was already on his way out, his mind determined. He might be pissed at his brother, but Gabe had a point. It was time he got Emma back. He wasn't taking no for an answer—and he sure as hell wasn't going to let Jake keep him from seeing her. Not this time. He was done with trying to be patient in the hopes she'd come around. And he was done waking up in an empty bed.

He needed her back in his life. He craved her, yearned for her touch, her body, and he missed her as if a piece of his soul, his heart had died. He couldn't think of anyone or anything but her, and he'd had enough. He had to fix this, had to get his life back. And the only way to do that was to get her to take him back.

It didn't take long to find himself impatiently pounding on Jake's door once more. It was late—but not so late that he'd be waking anyone. Eventually Jake answered the door, stepping out onto the porch and pulling the door shut behind him. "I need to speak to Emma—and I'm not leaving until I do. It's been three weeks, and I'm fucking tired of it."

Quinn expected Jake's usual rant about leaving her alone, about her not being interested, before it proceeded to Jake threatening to call the cops for trespassing, harassment, and stalking.

"She still doesn't want to see you, Ryker. And after what you put her through, you don't deserve her. Not one fucking iota. But…" Jake shook his head, and stuffed his hands in the pockets of his worn jeans. "But she's been miserable since you guys split. Even the prospect of rebuilding Old Port hasn't been enough to bring her around this past week. As much as I love her—and I do, make no mistake about it—I can't stand to see her like this."

It was one thing to suspect how Jake felt about Emma and another to hear it straight up. And though Quinn's jealous streak had him tightening a fist, he pushed it back, knowing damn well that Jake was the one thing standing between himself and Emma. "Then let me talk to her. For fuck's sake, I haven't spoken to her since this all happened."

"Just don't make me regret this, Ryker." Jake tilted his head towards the door and took a seat on the porch steps.

The tight ball of tension that'd been wound up in Quinn's chest finally started to slip free as hope washed over him. He let himself into the large home and immediately spotted Emma pacing in front of the fireplace. Fuck, it was so good to see her. And yet, he couldn't help but notice the dark circles under her eyes and the fact that she'd lost weight, her features more gaunt than he remembered them.

He'd done that to her. And he hated himself for it.

Desperate to hold her and make things right between them, he crossed to her side, only to have her take a step away from him. "What the hell are you doing here, Quinn?"

"Emma, please...I'm sorry. I'm sorry for hurting you, lying to you, and I'd find a million different ways to say it if it'd convince you that I truly meant it." He knew this was all his fault, but he needed her to forgive him. "Look, I know I fucked up, but it was never my intention to hurt you. It was just a situation that slipped out of my control. But I can't do this anymore. We need to find a way to get past this so you can come back home with me."

She shook her head and started to turn away when he grabbed her hand and pulled her to him, wrapping her in his arms and ignoring her struggles until they lessened and she leaned against him, her voice tight with emotion. "I can't do this, Quinn."

"Well, I'm not leaving, darling—and I'm not taking no for an answer. I need you, Emma—just like you need me." They were both miserable apart. That much was clear. "I meant it when I said that I love you. I can't bear not having you in my life, and I'll do whatever it takes to get you back."

Emma looked straight into Quinn's eyes. "I don't know how to get past this when I don't feel like I can trust you anymore. You lied to me, damn it. And all while preaching honesty. Not to mention, you knew how hard it was for me to trust you, given my past. To have you betray me? How the hell am I supposed to get past that?" Yet she hadn't pulled out of his arms, giving him the slightest glimmer of hope that she might give him another chance.

"I made a mistake, Emma." He cupped her cheek, and then, when she didn't pull away, he brushed her lips with a whisper of a kiss. "You know we're meant to be together. And damn it, Emma—I've never felt this way about anyone else. I'm not going to let you just give up on us."

He kissed her again and again, each kiss more demanding than the one before it. Tangling his fingers in her hair, his tongue found hers as she yielded to him, softening in his arms. It'd been weeks since he'd last touched her, held her, fucked her, and with her finally in his arms once more, he could think of nothing but getting her back home, where she belonged.

He nuzzled her, still trailing kisses over her skin as he spoke, unable to pull away. "Come home, darling… Let me make things right."

"Things can't just go back to the way they were, Quinn. That reality no longer exists—especially when I no longer have a restaurant or an income." There was so much emotion in her voice, he knew she was barely holding it together.

He'd wanted her new restaurant space to be perfect before he showed it to her, but that just wasn't an option at this point. He couldn't wait any longer. Not when she was so upset. "Come on then. There's something I need to show you."

"Quinn…"

He grabbed her hand and started pulling her towards the door. "I'm not taking no for an answer, darling. And you can either come along under your own steam, or I can haul your pretty little ass out of here with you tossed over my shoulder. Up to you, darling."

"You really are a pain in the ass." She shook her head and glared at him, though it only took another tug on his behalf to finally get her moving.

Jake got to his feet when they stepped out onto the front porch. "Em? You okay?"

She tossed Quinn a stern look before turning to Jake. "Yeah, I'm fine. We're just heading out for a bit, but I won't be long."

As Quinn pulled out onto the road, he was already feeling a million times more hopeful now that he had Emma at his side, as if she alone could make everything right in his world. And she could, because she was the only thing that mattered.

Steering them towards town, he couldn't help but reach over and link his hand with hers, before bringing it to his lips. "I've missed you, Emma. The last few weeks have been miserable without you. The house feels empty, the dogs are moping, and I can't even focus on work. You need to come home—our home. Tonight."

"That's not happening—and I'm not going to let you bully me into coming home with you." She yanked her hand free, some of her old spunk coming back.

He couldn't help but smile at her. "I don't want you to just come home, darling. I also want you in my bed. I've missed the way your body feels against mine, the way your body quivers when you come, and how you're always so wet for me, so willing. I love you, Emma. I love everything about you."

"Stop it, Quinn. I can't do this. And if you loved me, you wouldn't have lied to me." The emotion in her voice was impossible to ignore, and it killed him that he was the cause of her heartache. Yet he refused to let her question his love for her. Not when it was absolute.

"Don't, Emma. You don't get to question my love for you." That just pissed him off. How could she think he didn't love her? It was absurd. "I made a mistake—a big one that won't ever happen again—but it doesn't mean that I don't love you. I only wanted to protect you until I could get it sorted out."

Pulling up in front of the waterfront space he was renovating for her, he tossed the car in park. "What are we doing here?"

She'd find out soon enough. He went around to her side and grabbed her hand to help her out of the car. "Come on, sweetheart."

Late as it was, there was no one on the jobsite. He let them in, punched in the security code, and then flicked on some additional lights before turning to her.

"What is this place?" Emma's gaze shifted around the large space, taking it all in. The place had been transformed in the last few weeks, and though they were still a month away from completion, things were coming along nicely.

"It's your restaurant." He grabbed her hand, not quite sure what she was thinking or how she'd react once it finished sinking in. "I couldn't get out of the contract for your space, and with things held up due to the fire, I figured this was the next best thing. I know it's not your original location, but it's just around the corner from it. Not to mention, it has waterfront views, hard to come by parking, and there's outdoor seating. I've also got top-of-the-line equipment going in the kitchen, and I tried to match the décor and feel to what you had."

"Quinn…you can't just do this." She shook her head as tears threatened to spill over and slip down her cheeks. "This is really sweet of you, and I totally appreciate you doing this—the time, the effort, and especially the thought you put into it, but I can't afford this."

"You may not be able to, but I can—and I want to do this for you. I never meant for you to lose your restaurant, but I'm hoping this helps make up for it." He cupped her cheek and stole a gentle, lingering kiss, her lips sweet against his as she tentatively kissed him back after hesitating. "I was hoping to have it completed before showing it to you, but maybe this way, you can help me pick stuff out, so it's exactly the way you want it."

"This still doesn't fix your lies. I get that you didn't mean for things to turn out the way they did, but you should have talked to me about it. Instead you chose to lie and manipulate me." She shook her head and blinked away her tears. "How the hell am I supposed to get over that, Quinn?"

"I fucked up, Emma. I was just so scared of losing you, knowing that the only reason you were dating me was because of that lease. If I told you that I couldn't honor my promise to you, I knew you'd walk away from me." He ran a rough hand through his hair, all his worries and fears about losing her rising to the surface.

"It may have been the reason I agreed to see you in the first place, but you know it turned into so much more." She cursed under her breath. "You should have trusted me when I said that I loved you— and you should have trusted that by being honest with me, I'd see that you had done your best to save my restaurant."

"Emma...I'm sorry. I truly am. I know I fucked up, but you have to forgive me. I need you back in my life, and I'll be damned if I'm going to go another day without you by my side." The thought of them going their separate ways just wasn't an option. Not when he loved her so completely. "Please...don't push me away, love. Give me another chance. I know I can make you truly happy."

"You don't ever take no for an answer, do you?" She looked up at him with a stern look, tempting him to pull her close and brush her lips in another kiss.

"No, I don't. Not when it comes to you. You're stuck with me, darling, so you may as well get used to it." He tangled his fingers with hers and pulled her towards the back of the space where they'd started putting together the kitchen, relieved that she didn't put up a fight. "Come on, darling... Let me show you around."

He led her into the open kitchen area and flicked on some more lights, watching her as she took it all in. She wandered around the kitchen, most of the cooking equipment already in place. He'd had Finn come in and help him with the particulars, so that he could get all the details right.

She ran a hand over the stainless counter while looking at him, confusion darkening her eyes. "You did all this? For me?"

He closed the distance between them, desperate to touch her. "I'd give you the world if I could, darling, though I'll admit Finn did come over to make sure I wouldn't screw up the kitchen, since he knows grilled cheese is about the extent of my cooking skills. If there's anything you need changed, just let me know. I want this to be perfect for you."

When she turned to face him, he pulled her into his arms. "It *is* perfect. More than perfect. But I can't let you do this. It's too much, Quinn. And this does *not* mean we can just pick up where we left off, as if nothing ever happened."

"I'm not ignoring the fact that I fucked up, Emma. But it'll be a cold day in hell when I walk away from you. Or let you walk away from me. I love you—and you love me too. If you deny that, then you're doing nothing but lying to yourself." He brushed the hair from her face and cupped her cheek, looking into her hazel eyes, streaked with green and flecked with brown. "You need to give us another chance."

"Don't you think I want to? But I can't—even if I still love you. I can't pretend that everything's perfect between us, when I'm worried about being lied to again." She tried to pull away when her eyes glistened with tears, though Quinn just tightened his hold. "Let go of me, Quinn. Please..."

"Never, darling."

21

EMMA WANTED TO SCREAM. WANTED to pound on Quinn's chest until he let her go. Yet at the same time, she wanted him to kiss her until her anger melted away and he dragged her to his bed.

Curse him.

He was methodically weakening her resolve to stay angry with him. From his touch, his kisses, the restaurant… She'd never seen anyone be so thoughtful and generous, and though he had more than enough money so that he'd never feel the cost of the restaurant, she also knew he was damn busy. Too busy to be personally oversee-ing such a renovation.

And he was doing it all for her.

"I still can't accept the restaurant, Quinn, even if it's amazingly generous of you. It's no longer just me—I've agreed to let Jake become a partner in the restaurant." If Quinn was doing all this for her—and her alone—then he needed to know that Jake was now part of that equation.

"If that means you'll have less to worry about and you'll have more time on your hands, then that's fucking perfect as far as I'm concerned, since it means you'll have more time to spend with me. In our house, and in my bed." His gaze was so intense, it had her breath catching. And when he gripped her hips in a firm hold with both hands, she couldn't help but want him.

Dragging her to him, his mouth covered hers in a kiss, demanding, taking, his tongue thrusting past her lips to stoke her need for him and dampen her hurt and anger. She thought of pushing him away, telling him that it changed nothing. And yet it was the first time in weeks that she wasn't miserable.

His kiss deepened as he pinned her against the counter, making it impossible to ignore the hard length of his erection as it pressed against her in a not-so-subtle reminder of all the times he'd made love to her. And that's exactly what it'd been. It may have started as just sex, a release they both needed and enjoyed, but it'd quickly become so much more.

She couldn't deny him, couldn't deny what he meant to her.

He nipped at her neck, his thumbs brushing her breasts as his hands slipped up her waist, while her fingers tangled in his shirt, holding onto him as her head spun with need. "Fuck, Quinn…why do you do this to me?"

"Because I love you, Emma." Cupping her face in both his hands, he held her gaze, his eyes shifting for just a moment to her lips. "With everything that I am, I love you."

"I love you, too." And she did, damn him. When he smiled a shit-eating grin and kissed her again, she pulled away and slapped his chest. "But that does *not* mean everything's okay between us."

"As long as I get to make it up to you…" He trailed kisses and bites down her neck and across her jawline, sending a shiver through her, making her clit ache with need, desperate for release. "I promise to be good to you, darling. More than good. And I swear, by the time I'm through with you, you won't remember your own name, let alone why you were angry with me."

"Damn you, Quinn." And then he was kissing her again as she kissed him back, kissing him as if she needed him more than the air she breathed, kissing him as if he was the very beat of her heart.

He lifted her up onto the counter as she wrapped her legs around him, pulling him close, and when he spoke, his words drifted over her skin between kisses. "Let's go home, love. I've missed you..."

"I missed you too—but I can't go home with you. Not yet." Even though she wanted him desperately. "I just need a little more time to work back up to where we left off."

Already, he was looking at her like she was cornered prey and he was getting ready to devour her. "Fair enough—but I can't guarantee how patient I'll be."

"Why doesn't that surprise me?" She couldn't help but smile. And then she kissed him again, sweetly this time, cupping his face as she remembered something she'd been meaning to speak to him about. "Quinn...I wanted to thank you. Nate called to tell me you had taken care of his physical therapy and you'd set him up with an appointment to see a specialist. It was incredibly generous for you to do that, even after we'd split up."

He brushed her cheek and nuzzled her with a kiss. "I promised you I'd take care of getting him the help he needed. I wasn't going to break that promise too."

"You're a good man, Quinn." She couldn't keep the emotion out of her voice, her arms tightening around his neck as she held onto him, before finally managing to compose herself. "Come on. Show me the rest of the restaurant."

With his eyes locked on hers, he bit her lip, making her breath catch, and then helped her off the stainless-steel counter. "Happy to."

Slipping her hand in his, he took her through the whole restaurant, pointing out all the details—the long copper-topped mahogany bar, the leather cushioned booths, the hand-blown seeded glass light fixtures. There was a large patio with a wall of windows that could be opened when the weather was good, bringing the outdoors in. The details went on and on, all of it gorgeous, incredibly expensive, and more than anything, well thought-out.

Quinn had taken the time to really think of the space, her needs, the feel of the Old Port—and he'd nailed it. It felt like home—albeit a more expensive and upscale version of the place she'd loved. And he'd done it all for her.

Standing behind her as she looked out at the lights of the historic port glistening off the water, he slipped his arms around her waist and pulled her close, nuzzling her cheek before kissing it. "Do you like it, sweetheart?"

She pulled his arms tight around her and leaned back against him. "I love it, Quinn. I can't believe you did all this for me."

"I'd find a way to give you all the stars in the night sky if it would make you happy."

In that moment she knew…she knew it was the truth. Quinn loved her, absolutely and without limits. She had no more doubts. And if that were the case, then she had to believe that he would have saved her restaurant if it had been at all possible—and she had to believe that he'd never meant to hurt her.

"Can you take me home?" She spun in his arms to face him, her heart thundering against her chest, knowing it felt right despite everything. "To our home…"

He cupped her face in his hands and kissed her, his touch tender. "I'd love nothing more, darling."

With a quick text sent to Jake so he wouldn't worry, it didn't take long before they were making their way to Quinn's bed, shedding their clothes as fast as they could manage without tripping themselves up, one kiss leading to the next. Emma gasped when Quinn lifted her into his strong arms, his muscles tensing so they bulged, hard and firm, as he lowered her onto his bed.

"It's been too fucking long, love. Don't ever leave me again—I'd go insane." Kneeling on the mattress between her legs, he slid a hand up her thigh up to her panties, hooking them at the side and pulling them down, so she lay before him naked, the last of their clothes gone, as he lowered himself to her, capturing her mouth in a kiss.

Yet she managed to pull away long enough to get out the words that were nagging her, needing him to reaffirm where things stood, if they had any hope of truly moving past this. "Promise me there won't be any more lies, no more secrets. No matter what's happening in our lives, we deal with it together."

He pulled away enough to look at her, shifting his weight onto one elbow so he could cup her face, his gaze intense. "You have my word, Emma. I swear it to you. I love you. More than life."

"And you have mine." She had to choke back her tears, though this time, they were tears of relief. "I've never loved anyone the way I love you, Quinn."

He nuzzled her, nipping at her lips between kisses. Desperate to have him, to feel him claim her in the most primal of ways, she wrapped her legs around his waist, and pulled him close. He thrust into her with a needy growl, taking her fully and with such intensity, that she knew this wouldn't be a tender and slow coupling, but rather one that would push away all their fears, and banish the demons of their mistakes, linking them as one, body and soul.

Each thrust claimed her as his, and his alone, just as she claimed him, for there'd be no turning back from this moment for either one of them. He took her rough and hard, as if unable to hold back, unable to control what was between them, his fingers tangled in her hair as his pace picked up and his kisses deepened.

And then she was coming, crying out as her orgasm crashed through her, and he joined her with her name on his lips, his body tensing as his cock pulsed deep inside her, and they were finally reunited as one, all wrongs forgiven.

22

THE RING OF QUINN'S CELL phone tore through his blissful sleep, as he fumbled towards the night table with Emma still in his arms. Four a.m. Gabe. Something was wrong. It had to be. Gabe wouldn't be calling him at that hour otherwise.

"What's wrong?" Adrenaline had his heart racing, as Emma started to stir.

"It's Morgan." Gabe's voice was shaking, unsettled. "I was driving him home from the club when a car came out of nowhere and drove us off the road."

"Fuck. Is he okay—are you okay?" His thoughts were racing, trying not to think of the worst.

"I'm okay, just banged up, but Morgan's in surgery. They're not sure of the extent of his injuries, but they're hopeful he'll pull through." Gabe took a deep breath, anger in his voice. "It wasn't an accident, Quinn. They rammed us. Repeatedly. Just as we were going by the rocky cliffs. I think you were right about the fire not being about Emma."

Fuck. That made everything all the more dire—because it didn't look like the attacks would be ending anytime soon.

"We'll be right there." He was already throwing on jeans, and Emma was following suit. "Have you called Mom and Maddie?"

"Yeah. Mom's on her way and Maddie's flying in from London. Quinn…be careful. If these are the same people who started the fire, then this might be escalating."

Quinn hung up and wrapped his arms around Emma as she walked into his embrace, needing the comfort only she could give him. "You don't have to come, darling."

"We're in this together. No matter what happens, I want to be the one at your side. I want to be there for you. I love you, Quinn. Through the good and the bad."

He cupped the back of her neck and held her to him, pressing a kiss to her forehead, knowing beyond a doubt that this was the woman he wanted to wake up to every day, the woman he wanted to grow old with. "You're my heart, Emma, my soul, my everything."

"As you are mine."

The End

I hope you enjoyed *Seduction and Surrender. Submission and Surrender*, book two in The Billionaire's Temptation Series, is now available through all major retailers, including Amazon. Please read on for a sample, in addition to a sample of my romance, *One Sweet Summer,* the first in my Mermaid Isle Series. Hope you'll enjoy it, and for news on more new releases, please feel free to sign up for updates through my newsletter. http://calimackay.com

– Cali MacKay

Submission
AND SURRENDER

1

SITTING ALONE AT THE HOTEL bar, Hadley let out a ragged breath and wrestled with her emotions as she hung up with her lawyer, his words still echoing in her head. After two long years of legal wrangling, her divorce was final.

Tears stung her eyes, even though it felt like she could finally breathe again without the weight of her past sitting on her chest. Matt had been a lying, cheating bastard, and yet at one point they'd truly loved each other—or at least she'd thought they had. But that was before she'd lost herself in her work, taking on one case after another, and before Matt lost his job, started gambling away everything they owned and then cheated on her with some woman he'd met in therapy.

Trying to ignore the steady thump of loud music that made its way over the speakers, she took a long swig of her beer, thinking it ironic that she was a police consultant—a special investigator, no less—and yet she'd managed to ignore all the signs that'd been right under her nose. Part of her wondered if it'd just been easier for her to remain oblivious rather than to try to deal with a crumbling marriage.

And then Matt cleaned out her savings on a week-long excursion to Vegas with his girlfriend. That had been the slap in the face she'd needed.

They'd then spent the next few years with him promising to clean up his act and her hating him each time he'd lapsed back into his old habits. He'd refused to get help, and after she'd caught him cheating once more, that had been the last straw.

Vowing never to let love cloud her judgment again, she'd packed her bags and filed for divorce.

Two years ago.

Part of her felt as though she should be celebrating, but there was an even bigger part of her that felt like she'd failed. Failed to see the truth. Failed to keep her marriage together. Failed at being a wife.

The only thing she was good at was her job. And at this point, her job was the only thing she had left. Her cases. Solving her mysteries. At least she was making a difference by putting criminals behind bars and solving cases that had hit a wall.

She supposed she could blame her failed marriage on The Curse—the curse of the Moore women that always resulted in them picking shitty men. Her gran, her mom, her sister, *herself*...every one of them had been screwed over and messed around with.

She'd thought she'd picked a good one with Matt—and he *had* been a great husband at the beginning. He'd showed her what it was like to be happy, and he'd made her want that sort of a fairy-tale romance. And then the curse hit, and it all went down the stinking toilet after he got laid off and ended up with far too much time on his hands—time he'd spent gambling and then fucking other women when he was supposed to be getting help with his problem. At least they hadn't brought kids into that mess.

Knowing it'd be far too easy to let her past drag her down, Hadley vowed to make the most of this new start—this new life. She was finally free of her past and she could start fresh. Leave her mistakes and the curse behind. Find out who she really was when she didn't have baggage pulling her down into a pit of desperation and threatening to drown her.

With her eyes still on her beer, she felt the air around her shift as someone took a seat next to her. She barely needed a sideways glance to take in the details. Male, tall, far too much cheap cologne, and since there were plenty of other seats at the bar and he'd decided instead to crowd her, it meant that he was going to be a nuisance.

"I'll have what the pretty lady's having, and one more for her." To her, he said, "Name's Ryan."

Hadley let out a sigh, and shifted in her seat to face him, managing a small smile as she took him in. Too young, too built, too full of himself, and too drunk, if she had to guess. "I appreciate it, but I'm all set. Thanks."

"I'm just trying to buy you a drink, princess." Leaning against her, he closed in on her space, brushing her hair off her shoulder in a move that earned him a glare. "Can't a guy buy you a drink, or do you think you're too good for me? You haven't even told me your name."

"I think I'm done here." She didn't want to get into it, and he wasn't worth the aggravation. The only reason she was even at the hotel was because she was helping with a new case and it was too far from home for her to commute.

She slipped off the stool when he grabbed her arm. "Hey...where you going? I want to get to know you better. Have a bit of fun. Come on...stay and have a drink."

Why...why couldn't she just be left alone to wallow in her misery? She'd wanted a bit of a distraction, but not this. She yanked free of his grasp, fire in her eyes. "Buddy—touch me again, and you'll live to regret it."

"Ooo, spunky. I like that." Ryan got to his feet, and though she never thought of herself as short at five six, the guy was tall. And big. She could take care of herself, but he could easily pick her up off her feet and plant her. If she was a cop, she'd have a badge to scare him away with, but she wasn't. She was a consulting investigator, which meant no badge, no gun, no handcuffs. "Don't go... Someone so pretty shouldn't be alone. And I really like you. Don't you want to really like me too?"

Yep. Definitely drunk, which meant that there was no chance of successfully reasoning with him. With a jolt of adrenaline kicking into her system, she backed up a step—and right into a wall of muscle, her fear spiking as she wondered if he'd brought a friend.

The stranger stepped around her and put himself between her and the jerk harassing her. "She's not alone. Not anymore. And she's already told you she's not interested. Now take your drink and get the fuck out of here."

"I saw her first, so you can fuck off. Go find your own. This one's mine."

As big as Ryan was, the guy coming to her defense was just as big, if not bigger. And the way he moved—he might be muscular, but there was an ease in his movements that made her think he'd be quick and dangerous.

And he was. He dodged a blow, and before she could really see what was happening, her stranger had Ryan pinned to the bar with his arm twisted painfully around his back as he groaned in pain. "You need to leave, or I'm going to make sure you regret it. Are we clear?"

"Fuck...let go of me, man. I didn't mean anything by it." Ryan struggled to get free but it wasn't happening.

Her handsome stranger yanked him upright, though he'd yet to let go of Ryan's arm, twisting it so it was clearly painful. "Apologize to the lady for touching her."

"I'm sorry. Fuck...let go of me, man. That fucking hurts." He was set free with a shove that put plenty of distance between them, looking over his shoulder as he slunk back towards a dark corner on the other side of the bar.

"Thanks." Though Hadley could have probably taken care of the guy herself—with a whole lot of effort and no guarantees—it was damn nice not to have to. Especially when the guy coming to her aid was smoking hot. He was everything that other guy had tried but failed to be.

"Are you okay?" His worried gaze took her in, as he put a gentle hand on her arm and steered her away from the bar. Except that this time, she wasn't bothered by someone touching her. Not in the least.

"I am. Thanks for asking—and thanks for dealing with that asshole." Her heart was now racing for an entirely different reason. There was something about the guy standing in front her that made her crappy mood disappear.

He was damn good-looking, in a way that combined rugged and refined. His dark brown hair looked casually mussed like he'd been running his hands through it, and he had just enough stubble on his strong jaw to make his bright blue eyes stand out. Though he looked as though he could wear anything from flannel to a suit and look damn good in any of it, he'd continued that rugged yet refined theme by pairing worn jeans that fit him perfectly and a pair of scuffed Docs, with a navy cashmere sweater that hugged every muscle and fit him perfectly.

"My name's Hadley, by the way." She nervously tucked her hair behind her ear, and tried to remember the last time she'd attempted to flirt. It'd been ages. But if ever there was a time to attempt it, this would be it, given that gorgeous guys like the one before her *never* wandered into her life.

"Gabe. It's a pleasure." He tilted his head towards the other end of the bar with a disarming smile. "Not that you want a repeat, but can I buy you a drink? Or would you rather get out of here?" He ran a gentle finger down her cheek and leaned in just a little, lowering his head to hers so the air between them crackled with sexual tension.

Before meeting Gabe, she'd been ready to go back to her room and dig into the case file she'd just picked up the police station. But now? She was thinking that after such a crappy day, she could easily do with a distraction as good-looking as Gabe, especially since it'd been years since she'd let a guy get close.

Managing a flirty smile—at least she hoped it was flirty—she leaned into him and went onto the tips of her toes so she could whisper in his ear. "I think I'd like to get out of here—if you're up for it."

"Oh, I'm definitely up for it, sweetheart." He slipped his hand up the back of her neck and pulled her close, nuzzling her as he brushed her lips in a kiss that shot right through her and left her desperate for more.

She never did this sort of thing. *Never*. But hadn't she just been thinking that she wanted to start a new chapter in her life, and she wanted a change? Well, Gabe couldn't be any more perfect for kicking off her new life with a bang.

She no longer wanted to be the woman trapped in a bad marriage, or the woman who'd forgotten how to have fun. It'd been a long time since she'd felt any sort of happiness outside of a job well done, and she was still far too young to feel so defeated and dejected.

She needed this. She needed to forget her past, her failures, even if it was for just one night. And after feeling like she hadn't been good enough for an ass-wipe like Matt, she desperately needed to feel wanted, even if it was for something purely physical.

Slipping a strong arm around her shoulder, Gabe held her close as he led them out of the bar and into the hotel lobby, his hard body pressed against hers as if giving her a preview of what was to come. She couldn't quite believe she was going to do this, and she hated to admit it, but her nerves were getting the better of her, her heart racing like it might jump out of her chest.

"You seem nervous, sweetheart." He slowed them to a stop and pulled her close, his grip on her hips firm enough to ramp her excitement up another notch. "Anything I can do to help?"

"Yeah...kiss me." This was a fresh start, a new her, and she refused to overthink it. She needed this. More than anything.

"Happy to, babe." Cupping her face, he knotted his large hands in her hair and dragged her up to him, covering her mouth in a kiss that was sweet yet passionate enough to have her breath catching. His tongue darted past her lips as his kiss deepened, causing her clit to throb with a heavy pressure that begged for release. He pulled away, but only for a moment before dragging her back to him and biting her bottom lip, his words spoken against her skin on a needy breath. "Fuck...I want you, Hadley."

With her heart hammering inside her chest, she hooked her fingers through the loops of his jeans and pulled his hips to her, making it impossible to ignore his long, hard length—and damn if that didn't make him all the more irresistible. "It's been a really long time since anyone's wanted me."

"That's just so fucking wrong, sweetheart."

End of Sample. *Submission and Surrender* is now available for purchase. Please read on for a sample of *One Sweet Summer*, a novel by Cali MacKay.

One Sweet Summer

A MERMAID ISLE ROMANCE

CHAPTER *One*

R ILEY FOUGHT TO TAKE A breath, the news hitting her like a sucker punch to the gut, her world crumbling out from under her. "You can't sell the inn. It's the heart of the island. It's my home."

She knew business had slowed with the downturn in the economy, but they'd managed to stay profitable, even if the numbers were down. She'd hosted conferences and booked more weddings, kept the numbers up for the artist retreats, and even held treasure hunts for the legendary Mermaid Isle pirate treasure. They'd all busted their butts to make sure the inn stayed afloat. It was just a rough patch they'd need to ride out, but they'd been through worse and managed to pull through.

"Riley, you've done an amazing job running the place, and it's because of you that we've managed to hold on as long as we have. But the roof will need to be replaced in the next year or two, and the entire place needs to be updated. We just don't have the money to keep up with everything that's needed, and the truth is, we're getting old. We want to retire while we're still young enough to enjoy it." Jack reached over and took Ava's hand, giving her a smile. Married forty years and still in love like they were teenagers.

She could only be so lucky to find love like that someday.

Ava's easy smile could normally part the grayest clouds, yet today, it did little to take the edge off Riley's nerves. "We weren't looking to sell just yet, but we got an offer out of the blue. We couldn't refuse, Riley, but we negotiated your position into the sale, so you'll have nothing to worry about. You have the option to continue working at the Siren Song Inn or you can take the generous severance package they're offering. We're hoping you'll stay, though. It'll be easier for us to leave the place if we know you'll still be here to take care of it."

At least she could still stay if she wanted to. Not that it would be the same with Jack and Ava gone and new owners at the helm. They'd want to change it. Turn it into another cookie-cutter hotel. Gone would be her artist's collective and the herbalist conference. And who knew what they'd do with the century-old cottages.

Maybe if it was an individual or a couple rather than some corporation. They might stand a chance then. "Who's bought the Siren?"

As if reading her thoughts, Jack frowned. "Holt Enterprises. They're big, but promised to let you take the lead on the changes they'll be making."

Yeah...and dreams were made of cotton candy and gumdrops. She bit back a groan, not wanting to make this anymore difficult on Jack and Ava than it already was. "Where will you go?" Now that she'd made Mermaid Isle her home, she couldn't imagine living anywhere else.

"Honey, another Maine winter will do us in." Jack sat back and laughed. "I want sun and warm waters. Sandy beaches that I can walk on without getting swept out to sea. Drinks I can sip out of a coconut or pineapple and are loaded up with rum."

Riley wanted to protest that they could have those things here, but knew it wasn't the same. And Jack was right—the winters could be harsh this far north, even if they were still in the southern part of Maine.

"Might do a bit of traveling before we settle down." Ava looked at her, her motherly concern still worrying her brown eyes. "But we'll come back during the summers. And we'll stay in touch. We'll only be a phone call or email away—not to mention all the current technology. What's it called? Swipe?"

That made Riley laugh. "The world must be coming to an end then, if I'm going to finally get you two to go online and actually answer emails."

"You'll manage just fine, my dear." Ava got to her feet and Jack followed suit. "If anything, you might finally get the funds to do all those things you've been wanting to do here at the Siren. Change is good."

"When? When will the sale be finalized?" Riley's breath hitched as she waited for an answer. She'd come here every summer as a child, worked at the inn during her vacations once she'd turned eighteen, and then full-time straight out of college. It was where she'd grown up, where she'd fallen in love for the first time. It was all she knew, all she loved—and she'd given it her all.

"In two weeks. And don't worry—we'll tell the others." Ava gave her a big hug. "Just remember, this will always be the Siren Song Inn. As long as you're here, the heart of it will never change."

"I hope you're right." She couldn't bear to think of the Siren changing so much it no longer felt like home.

Riley waited for Jack and Ava to leave her office and then collapsed into her chair, tears stinging her eyes as she tried to swallow down the golf ball-sized lump in her throat. She knew they'd been looking to retire, but she hadn't expected them to sell the place. Not that she held it against them—all their money was tied up in the inn, and they'd never be able to retire without freeing up those funds.

She thought of what the Siren meant to so many people. Cultivated over the years to be an artist's retreat, there was a long list of people who came year after year to meet with other like-minded folks, and be inspired by the rugged natural beauty and colorful town.

Unlike other places that catered only to the rich and well off, Mermaid Isle was more approachable and far more unique than any other resort town Riley had ever been to, especially given its long history. Legend had it that thieves and pirates had stashed their plunder in one of the many caves that could be found on the island, and later, it was settled by a small group of women who'd come north to escape the witch trials that reached far past Salem. Add to that the commune that blossomed in the sixties and the artisans that flocked to it in the last few decades, and it would be impossible to duplicate the character of the island and its people.

But with the Siren under new ownership, everything might change, and it could easily devastate the island's economy. There were a handful of small bed and breakfasts, but the inn was at the heart of the island and it was their constant influx of guests that kept the money flowing—guests that could appreciate the island's quirky nature.

She'd just have to make sure she held onto the reins. There was more at stake than just the inn or her job.

Checking the time, she went to the front desk and grabbed the keys to the van, hoping that the drive into town would help clear her head. "I'll go grab the next group of visitors coming in on the ferry."

Logan gave her a small frown, his blue eyes filled with worry, though handsome as he was, he even made devastation look good. He stepped away from the front counter where'd he'd been dealing with some paperwork, and pulled her into a hug, kissing the top of her head. "I just heard. I'm really sorry, Riley. But it could be good, right?"

She managed a smile, knowing it was important to stay positive for the troops. Slipping out of the comfort of his arms, she did her best to push her concerns and apprehensions aside. "Exactly. Everything will work out fine. And just think of all the things we can do if we have a bit of money coming in. Might finally be able to give the rooms that remodel we've been dreaming of."

She'd have to make it work. Failure wasn't an option—not when there was so much on the line. She'd put far too much of herself into the inn to have it all go to hell. And if Holt Enterprises thought they could just come in and bulldoze everything she'd worked so hard to build and care for, then they had better get ready for a fight.

Stay positive, she reminded herself. It didn't have to be all doom and gloom. Holt might only make a few changes while providing a good infusion of much-needed cash to remodel the place.

With new plans and ideas running through her head, Riley drove the van down to the center of town, taking in the late summer sun and the bustling shops as she made her way to the port. It really was a special place, the brightly colored shingled cottages playing up against the blue sky and sea, while riots of flowers poured out of window boxes. She pulled up by the landing just as the ferry docked and started to unload its passengers. Perfect timing.

There were two ways to get to Mermaid Isle. There was a ferry that left Portland and was convenient for those guests coming from Boston or other points south, and then there was a bridge that connected the island to the mainland an hour north of Portland. During the summer, most opted for the ferry. Some even brought their cars, though most made do with the hotel's bikes or rented a scooter from a shop in town. But in the winter time, Riley usually recommended the bridge since the winter seas could be rough and unpredictable, and service was limited.

With the hotel's name emblazoned on the side of the van, she waited for her group to arrive, clipboard in hand. One newlywed couple, three writers who'd signed up for their Romancing the Isle writer's workshop, and two other individuals who had booked separately. Watching the crowds come in off the ferry, Riley knew there would be a fair number of people who would day-trip it, and take the evening ferry home, but it was the ones who stayed, even just a night or two, who usually came back time and again.

A group of women, ranging from their forties to sixties, laughed and chatted their way off the boat and wandered over, wide-brimmed straw hats atop each head and sundresses flowing in the summer breeze. Her romance writers—the ones who had been to the inn previously and decided to add a few days to their workshop by coming early. "Welcome to Mermaid Isle. Jan, Pat, Diane—so nice to see you again."

One after another, the trio gave her a big hug. Pat took the lead. "Not a chance in hell we'd miss this workshop. And I hope you still have that cutie, Logan, working for you. He's the inspiration for my next hero. Tall, dark hair, those blue eyes—not to mention that build."

Jan nudged her friend. "You haven't stopped talking about him since we were last here. Riley, you best warn the poor man. This one here's up to no good. She'll be dropping things left and right just to get him to bend over and pick them up."

Riley had to smile, her worries drifting away on the women's laughter. She leaned over for a mock whisper. "Well, he does have a nice butt, but don't tell him I said so or I'll never hear the end of it."

"I don't know what you're waiting for, honey. If it were me, I'd be trying out a new scene every night of the week with him in the leading role." Diane threw her head back and laughed, before turning to the other writers. "That man is book cover material."

Riley would *not* tell them that she'd dated Logan on and off, knowing the writers would attempt to get them back together, when they were better off just being friends.

Pat put a hand on Diane's arm. "Don't go forgetting the rest of them. What were their names?"

Diane shrugged with a laugh. "Couldn't tell you. My eyes weren't on their nametags."

The writers laughed their way onto the bus as a good-looking couple in their early thirties approached and introduced themselves. "Ken and Emma Murray."

Riley welcomed them to the island and checked them off her list when her attention was pulled in a completely different direction. Given the constant stream of visitors they got on the island, there weren't many men who could have her doing a double-take, but damn if this one didn't have her heart forgetting how to beat properly. And he was walking towards her, his long stride eating up the distance between them.

The man was…tall. And…words failed her. Despite the cotton tee and worn jeans, he looked like a Viking god, his honey-colored hair just long enough to make a girl want to run her fingers through it, his strong jaw covered in several days' growth. There was an ease to his step and demeanor despite his muscular build, like he was comfortable in his body and knew how to use it.

He shifted the large duffel he was carrying and gave her a smile that had her blushing, while his blue eyes held her captive in his gaze. "Hey there, darling."

Darling, eh? She liked it. *And* he had an accent—something European. Well-schooled and definitely English but with a little bit of something else thrown in.

"Welcome to Mermaid Isle." Her heart nearly stuttered along with her mouth. She glanced at her clipboard. The name wasn't familiar, but there was something about him...those eyes, the accent. And there was only one person who'd ever had such an immediate effect on her. "Thorsen Black?"

"That would be me." His smile kicked up a notch, his gaze making her feel like she was the only person there. "And you could only be Riley. Riley Carter."

"That's me. Have you been to the Siren Song Inn before?" She must have had her head stuck in a hole to not notice him the last time he'd come to the inn. Even the writers were opening the windows on the bus and jostling for a better view.

"You don't remember me, do you?" The humor in his smile had her wondering when they'd last met. "Think back to when we were teenagers. You got yourself stuck on the cliff..."

"Oh, god..." She squeezed her eyes shut and cringed.

That had been one of the most embarrassing moments of her life, and one she thought she'd left behind along with her braces and training bras. Memories of that summer flooded her head as she thought of the teenage boy who'd saved her that day. He'd ended up being her first true love—and *her first*. But...she looked at the name. It was different to what she remembered.

He must have seen her confusion. "I used to go by my middle name back then—Eirik."

Eirik Black. That was the name she remembered.

How often had she thought of him over the years? Maybe it was because their summer together—and the one after that—had been magical and he'd been the first guy she'd fallen in love with. But it seemed like no other relationship ever came close to measuring up. Not even the good ones.

"I can't believe it's you." With her heart racing erratically, she gave him a quick hug, not quite believing Eirik—Thorsen—was standing in front of her. "How have you been?"

"Good. You?"

Someone cleared their throat, keeping them from reminiscing further. Riley turned to find the last person on her list. "Anna Blake?"

"It is." A smile graced her face for no more than a second before fading to a no-nonsense demeanor.

"Well…welcome to the island." Riley managed a smile, though the woman before her didn't exactly inspire the warm and fuzzies.

Though everyone had their own sense of style, Anna's outfit didn't exactly say summer vacation—business attire head to toe, the woman looked like she was a lawyer. Dark suit jacket, even in the middle of summer, paired with a slim skirt and white blouse, heels that looked better suited to Manhattan than Maine, and blonde hair that was perfectly styled and probably cost hundreds to cut and an hour to style. They hadn't scheduled any corporate events, since most of their summer business came from vacationing tourists.

Riley got a sinking feeling in the pit of her stomach as she re-checked the name on her list. Anna Blake. There was no company listed near her name. Not that there would be. She managed another smile, though she couldn't help but wonder if Anna was from Holt Enterprises. "That's everyone. If you'd like to grab a seat on the bus, we'll get going."

Thorsen stepped to the side to let Anna go first, leaving them alone for the moment—if one didn't count the gaggle of romance writers watching their every move. He was only inches away and giving her a smile that had her toes curling, her breath catching, and her pulse doing cartwheels. "I know you'll be working, but I'd love to get together and catch up. It's been ages."

She melted into those blue eyes, her gaze darting to those lush lips of his as her mind and body vividly imagined what it would be like to kiss him after all these years. Giving him a smile, she managed to concentrate long enough to give him an answer, though her voice came out all breathy, betraying the effect he was having on her. "I might be able to swing that."

CHAPTER *Two*

THORSEN COULD BARELY PULL HIS gaze away from Riley long enough to take in the island. As a seventeen-year-old boy, he'd been absolutely smitten with her, head over heels in love, and their two summers together nowhere near long enough.

And now? He was in no better shape than he'd been back then. The feelings he'd once had for her seemed to hit him like a runaway train, though he wondered if they'd ever really left him. Perhaps he'd just tucked them away in a safe place, knowing that until now, his life was too chaotic to accommodate anything more than a quick hook-up.

And Riley sure as hell was *not* just hook-up material.

She'd been sweet and cute when they'd been teens, but now she was nothing short of a natural beauty. Her long dark brown hair caught the sun so it shone with shades of red, and freckles danced across her cheeks, making her green eyes sparkle. His only regret was that he'd lost track of her after their last summer together. They'd tried to stay in touch, but Thorsen had been sent back to England to finish his last year of boarding school. The heavy workload and the strict school rules hadn't allowed for many distractions.

Well, this time around, he wasn't going anywhere. He'd spent the years since that last summer thinking about her, wanting her— replaying their one time together over and over in his head, their intimate moment stolen the night before he flew back home to England. There may have been others since then, but he knew no one else would truly do.

He'd dated plenty, but they'd been nothing more than a way to keep his mind off Riley. How many times had he thought of tracking her down? It would have been simple enough to do, and yet she would have been nothing but a temptation he couldn't pursue, given the work he'd been doing for Interpol. Any sort of serious relationship would only have put her in jeopardy, and that wasn't a risk he'd been willing to take.

But now? He'd switched gears professionally, and that meant he could finally think of settling down to a normal life, and go after the one and only thing he'd ever wanted—Riley.

A wave of memories hit him as they rounded the corner in the road and he saw it off in the distance. The Siren Song Inn. The sprawling estate was just as he remembered it.

Originally built during the late eighteen hundreds as a summer getaway and health resort, it had changed very little from its original blueprint. Painted a cheery yellow with white shutters and trim, the Siren was made picture-perfect with flower boxes added to every window while the sea and sky served as an ever-changing backdrop. A farmer's porch wrapped all the way around the building, and rocking chairs afforded the guests a place to sit, so they could enjoy the view with their company. It was everything one could want in a summer resort.

And yet it was so much more.

Though he hadn't been at the helm of the family business long, Riley and the Siren Song Inn had never left his mind for long. Fueled by his memories of the perfect summers he'd spent on Mermaid Isle, it didn't take long for Thorsen to convince the other board members that it would be a sound investment. Days later, they'd made a generous offer on the Siren.

The fact that Riley was the manager seemed serendipitous. If he'd had any doubts as to whether or not to buy the quaint inn by the cliffs, that was enough to have him signing on the dotted line.

Not that Riley could know he was the head of Holt Enterprises—not yet anyway. Given his complicated dealings with Interpol, only the members on the board and a handful of lawyers knew of his standing and his involvement at Holt. And, he'd like to make sure it stayed that way. Though he might no longer be actively working with Interpol, it made little difference to the enemies he'd made over the years.

Not even Anna Blake knew she was sitting on the bus with one of her bosses—though what exactly she was doing on the island remained to be seen. He suspected his cousin, Mark, was behind it.

Mark had been hoping Thorsen would remain a silent partner, so he could gain control of Holt. Unfortunately, his cousin had been sorely disappointed, and given that they'd never liked each other much to begin with, the tension between them had only grown in the last few months.

Buying the inn had been a controversial move, but it would be even more so if it didn't soon turn a nice profit. Though Thorsen held controlling interest in Holt, he still had board members to appease, and the last thing he wanted was a coup—one Mark would happily lead with torches and pitchforks.

Having inherited his position in the company, every business decision he made was being questioned and scrutinized, and too many unhappy board members could mean losing control of his family's company. He owned the largest percentage compared to the other members; however, their sum total could override him in a decision. It was a precarious position to be in.

The bus pulled to a stop, though Thorsen held back and let everyone else get off first with the hope of getting Riley to himself, even if for a moment. A trio of women ogled him quite blatantly, but he just had to smile, flattered. Once he and Riley were the last two on the bus, he moved towards the exit where she stood.

She gave him a tentative smile. "I'm afraid you might get more of that...we've got a romance writer's conference going on, and let's just say, the ladies like their leading men and have a wild imagination."

He barked out a laugh. "That explains it then. Do you do a lot of that sort of thing here at the inn?"

"It helps keep the place full. We've managed better than most places with the slow economy, but…" Worry clouded over her eyes and her shoulders slumped, though she was quick to recover. "It's all good. This place has been around too long to not adapt and survive."

"I'm glad to hear it." He smiled and followed her off the bus.

Several inn employees were there to help them with their luggage and to check them in, and it didn't take long before he had his key card in hand. He lingered until she had a free moment, still desperate to talk to her some more. "I know you're busy, but I don't suppose I could interest you in dinner? Maybe tonight—unless you already have plans. It's been far too long, Riley."

"Tonight?" Mulling it over, she bit her bottom lip, making him want to kiss her.

"It's just dinner between old friends, darling." He was now worried she'd say no. "We could do it another night if you need to check with your boyfriend—or are you not supposed to mingle with the guests?"

That got him a laugh. "No boyfriend to check in with, and given that I'm here twenty-four-seven, my social life would be a black hole if I couldn't hang out with the guests. But work's a bit complicated right about now."

"Go on, Riley! Let the poor man take you to dinner." One of the romance writers nudged her while passing by, though the group of writers didn't look like they were going anywhere in a hurry.

He could see her mulling it over, and it left his gut in knots. After wanting her all these years, she had to say *yes*. "You still have to eat, right? Maybe leaving work behind for an evening is exactly what you need."

"Well, dinner usually consists of me grabbing something on the run between events we're hosting or while doing paperwork." Looking down, she laughed and shook her head. "I know—it's sad, isn't it?"

It was clear Riley poured everything she had into running the inn, and probably never stopped or slowed down enough to take a moment for herself. "All the more reason to say yes."

The light in her eyes had his heart pounding against his chest, making him want to steal the kiss that was over a decade too late. And then the romance writers backed him up once more, urging Riley on until she rolled her eyes at them with a smile. "You're right. Someone else can run this place for a night and dinner would be... *really nice.* Seven in the lobby?"

"Sounds perfect." He grabbed his bag and wandered towards the stairs, pausing for a moment at the group of women. "My sincerest thanks, ladies."

They were all giving him mischievous smiles that made him think it'd be good to have the writers as allies. "It's our pleasure."

He noticed Anna lingering, her lips pursed and her gaze stern as she took note of his exchange with Riley. It left him wondering if the board decided to send Anna to evaluate the hotel so they could decide on what changes they'd need to make. But Anna could be a huge problem for him since the board had made it quite clear that he was *not* to come to the island until their lawyers closed the deal on the inn. According to the board, inheriting his family's share of the business did *not* mean he'd also inherited their business sense.

Mark and the board may have hoped to continue running things, but it didn't sit well with him. He may not have an MBA, but he was far from being an idiot. And if they were purchasing the Siren because of his interest in it, then he wanted to make his own assessment of the place—whether they wanted him here or not. He wouldn't interfere, and they wouldn't know he was here.

It was why he'd been forced to lie to Riley about his name. She'd been right—Eirik was his first name, while Thorsen was one of the names he often used while working with Interpol. It'd be simple enough for someone to put the surnames together, but Black wasn't exactly unusual, and it'd be too hard to explain a different surname to Riley. In just a few weeks, the sale would go through and he'd tell her everything.

End Of Sample. *One Sweet Summer* is available for purchase through all major retailers."

MORE BOOKS BY CALI MACKAY

The Mermaid Isle Series
One Sweet Summer
For Love or Treasure
Sweet Danger

The Billionaire's Temptation Series
Seduction and Surrender
Submission and Surrender
Love and Surrender
Deception and Surrender (with more to come…)

The Highland Heart Series
The Highlander's Hope
A Highland Home
A Highland Heist

The Pirate and the Feisty Maid Series
(Parts One, Two, and Three)

Jack—A Grim Reaper Romance